DEVON L
Please return/renew th
Renew on tel. 0345 155 1001 or at
www.devonlibraries.org.uk

I was there –
I think

Biku Ghosh

D565656 1 889500

All rights are reserved, including the right to reproduce this book or portions thereof without the author's express written permission. This book is a work of fiction based on the author's personal reflections. Names and characters are the product of the author's imagination. Any resemblance to actual persons, living or dead, and families are entirely coincidental.

To

Laura and Julie

Human beings are members of a whole,
in creation of one essence and soul.
If one member is afflicted with pain,
other members uneasy will remain.
If you have no sympathy for human pain,
the name of human you cannot retain.

(Bani Adam - a 13th-century Persian poem by Saadi Shīrāzī)

Introduction

'Memory is the diary we all carry with us,' Oscar Wilde wrote.
But unlike photography and a written diary, memory does not 'capture' the past and sometimes disappears for unknown reasons.

In this collection of sixteen fictional short stories and one poem, the author takes a personal journey and sets the stories through generations and multiple continents. The principal theme of this collection is looking at a humane yet colourful world, in case we forget. The stories are written with empathy and emotion but hopefully not over-sentimental. Some stories highlight the issues an average woman faces daily in our world and the challenges to rise above them. This book may not bring social change, but hopefully, it might make us examine some of its essential issues.

The first story in this collection, *The dive*, was based upon the author's experience working as

a volunteer in Leonard Cheshire Disability Care home in Wales. There he came to know several people with severe disabilities but with interesting stories to be told from their earlier lives. During his mountaineering trips in the Himalayas, the author came across a sherpa with whom he became a friend. Both kept in touch for a few years through email. Unfortunately, all contacts were suddenly lost after the 2015 earthquake in Nepal. *The climber* story is dedicated to his memory.
The Coffee pot and *It's my husband's fault* stories are based on the author's extensive experience working in rural Ethiopia for over two decades. *It's my husband's fault* story is based upon an accurate reflection of the training programme as part of the Wales-based two decades of healthcare link with southern Ethiopia. Some sections of the story were published in medical journals (The Lancet 2015 & African Journal of Midwifery and Women's Health 2017). *The Choice* is based upon the author's chance to become friends with a driver during his volunteering visit to The Gambia. He was fortunate to be invited to the driver's family home, learn about their daily life and struggle, and later come across many in a similar situation.

The RAF pilot piece is from a collection of fictional stories from the author's earlier book,

'Indian immigrant.' This tells a story not as an offshoot of race relations but from the immigrant's perspective of working for and living in Britain. The author worked in a rural Australian town for two years and was involved in training Aboriginal healthcare workers. *The Queen* story is based on his visit to the Northern Territories. Only the names have been changed to protect the individual's privacy. The other story, also based in Australia, *Sharing the grief of a loss*, reflects actual events soon after the author's personal tragedy.

During his recent days as a community volunteer, the author befriended and supported several individuals with dementia. The title story, *I was there - I think*, and *Anniversary*, both are recollections of precious memories from working with some of them. *The Cricket Lover* was written following an encounter with a lady in her seventies with early dementia. She had followed the Indian Cricket team in many places over the years, including at the world cup final in Australia. *Bluebell woods*, the only poem in this collection, reflects the author's personal experience of knowing the families of several patients with cancer.

While volunteering as a medic in many countries, the author witnessed the inequalities and injustices in health care for ordinary people. Two stories in *Money over health* are based on real-life experiences working in India and Bolivia. In 2016 the author worked in several hospitals as a volunteer surgeon in Bolivia. *The handkerchief* recalls his pleasant memory of gratitude from one of his patients. *The twins* story was conceived following his visit to an orphanage in Bermejo, Bolivia. *Death of a humanitarian* is a sad but accurate description of the author's experience of knowing a volunteer doctor in Sierra Leone, who unfortunately passed away.

In 2017, the author suffered a sudden massive brain haemorrhage, from which he recovered completely a few months later. The ending story in this collection, *In another life*, is based on his personal experience and what could easily have been the other outcome.

These stories often occur in distant places but are still within the boundaries of our earth. Some of them are dark, and many have tragic sides, but they make you feel human and even are comforting. The author does not touch up people he likes but does not hide his hatred for injustices. Some of the issues this collection raises are often provocative and controversial, but his sympathies are clear. All sixteen stories have different points of interest but are bound by a collective theme of humanity, taking the reader through life simply as it is.

Growing up in an Indian village as the son of a doctor who chose to work in the villages to help the people in need, the author had the perfect beginning to look at this world with empathy. Always a voracious reader, the author was absorbed early in the short stories by Syed Mujtaba Ali, a Bengali writer cum travel enthusiast and world-famous Rabindranath Thakur. Soon after mastering enough English, his second language, the author was hooked on translated short stories by Fyodor Dostoevsky, the Russian short-story writer, French writer Guy de Maupassant and later Albert Camus, an Algerian-born French author.

'As you get older, three things happen. The first is your memory goes, and I can't remember the other two,' said Norman Wisdom.

At over seventy-five years of age, the author wants to share some of his precious memories told in these short stories with the readers before they are forgotten and lost forever.

Contents

The dive	12
The climber	26
The coffee pot	55
It's my husband's fault	68
The choice	77
RAF pilot	91
The Queen	104
Sharing the grief of a loss	118
Bluebell woods	124
I have been there – I think	127

Cricket lover	154
Money over health	
Khichan. Rajasthan	173
Yacouiba. Bolivia	185
Death of a humanitarian	191
The twins	198
Handkerchief	207
Anniversary	212
In another life	250

The dive

Wales 2014

I can easily press the bell, but for now, I don't want to.

My catheter bag has reached a bursting point and should be changed. Piss will be all over my bed otherwise, as only a couple of weeks before. I know the carer would be here immediately if I pressed the buzzer attached to my bed with a cord, but I want to be alone for now. Being alone has been my life for the last six years since I ended up in this place. I only want to drift in my past a bit longer this afternoon.

Heavy morning clouds have now completely disappeared. The scorching sun is boring down from the pale blue sky onto the turquoise sea below. The magical sea tantalises us with its dirty green colour of the reefs and then more with the circles of lighter shades of green near the cay. Pacific 2, moored close to the pristine white sandbar about ten nautical miles from the shore, bobs along gently in the calm wave. It's only late morning now, but the temperature is already close to forty degrees. As many passengers have already done, the crew would have preferred taking off their sweat-drenched tee shirts with the company logo too, but it's against the rule!

There is always that thrill of taking new learners underwater for their maiden scuba dive, even after doing this for more than five years. Loud chatter and shrills of about fifteen or so snorkelers jumping into the sea come from the stern side of the boat. Today I have only five beginners to take down with me, which should be easy. All of them are high with trepidation and thrill while struggling to put on the dive suits, some for the first time in their lives. The scuba tanks have been checked already and waiting by the bow side railing in a neat row to be attached to the divers.

Black inflatables attached by yellow cords to the ship are invitingly calm and, at the same time, spunky. All five novices with me have learned the safety signs earlier from us.

'Alex, can you show us the sign if you have a problem with equalising in your ear?' I ask.

He makes an open hand with his palm down, fingers apart, rocking back and forth while pointing to his ear.

'Excellent. Ellie?' I look towards a blonde girl who must be still in her teens.

'Ally,' she giggles.

'Sorry. Ally, can you show us how to tell me that you want to come up?'

She makes a fist with the thumb pointing up while moving her hand upwards.

'Brilliant, you all are a smart lot. Unless any of you have any questions, let's go and have some fun under the water now.'

Guessing the right weight for each one's belt and then strapping them with their scuba tanks while keeping an eye on all of them putting on their gears has been routine for me over the years.

Everyone has already checked out their flippers for sizes.

'No, no, don't put on your flippers until you are in the zodiacs and ready to dive!'

We get into our inflatables and sail into the sea about a hundred metres away from the large ship on the other side of the cay. All excited but nervous faces in front of me. I have decided to take them for their first dive, walking in from less than two metres in the water towards the slope of greater depth. Almost like teaching in a swimming pool for me, but it's a lot more exciting for them to be in the open sea in their diving gear. There is usually less panic this way than going straight into more depth.

'Put on your flippers, guys,' *I say as I switch off the inflatable engine and come to a stop.*

'Now, can you all sit with your backs towards the water on the side of the boat? Three on the port side and two with me on the starboard side. Put your regulators in your mouth,' *I say and then, watching one of them struggling with it, I move over to him.*

'Your both lips go over it, Andy, like this,' I demonstrate to him.

'Jump only one at a time when I call your name.' Then I jump from the boat first, waiting for them, and call.

Plop goes the first one into the water and then the other.

Knock at my door.

'Come in,' I say unenthusiastically.

'Rog love, Teatime soon. Do you want yours in the lounge with the others? I will get Sam to push you up there if you want,' my carer Angie, a curvy twenty-odd-year-old with a face to die for, asks as she looks through the door.

'I will have mine in my room, please.'

It has been a perfect day. Snorkelers and the divers have been happy. After taking photographs after photographs of themselves, with their new friends and with the crews, chattering loudly, they walk through the pier towards the shore. Tidying up the boat and getting everything ready for the next day has taken another half an hour or so for us, the crew.

All my mates, the other divemaster and most of the crew then had a good time at our favourite seaside bar for a couple of hours in the lazy warm evening. There was the usual banter in the thick smoke of the crowded room.

'Barry could not get away from that gorgeous blonde taking off her dive suit,' says someone.

'He was almost ready to give her a hand,' says another with a wicked smile on his face.

Barry just flashes his teeth. They usually spare me from such leg-pulling, most being much too junior to me. I also have some repute, as a few learned the trade from me.

'Sssh, the match is starting,' shouts a few from the other corner with a small table in front ready with several large glasses of beer.

EPL live match on the big screen comes on. Strange to see so many red supporters in this country, probably more than in the UK. Not my scene. Time to go home now.

I light my third cigarette and shout, 'I am off now, folks. Barry, are you ready?'

We drive off in my old sky-blue Renault.

****

I feel wet and sticky. I try to roll out of my bed but cannot move. My head hurts like hell. I realise I have wet myself and my pants are dirty too. Disgusted, I want to get up. I can only wriggle my right side. In frustration, I try to bring my hands close to my face. I can see my right hand, but the left one stays put with my left leg. It feels a ton in weight. I go back to sleep.

When I wake up again, a Thai nurse is standing over me.

'How are you doing, Mr Roger?' she asks in broken English.

I try to answer that my head hurts but can only mumble as saliva drips from the corner of my mouth.

In the next few weeks, I learn that I had a stroke. I would not be alive but for Barry. Running late to be picked up, Barry had tried to telephone me without luck. Fortunately, his flat was only a couple of blocks from mine. The car was in my drive, but no answer after knocking on the door for a few minutes had alarmed him to call for help. They had broken down the door to find me on the floor, and an ambulance was called immediately.

'Thank God you are alive. I honestly thought you were a gonner,' Barry says.

In the first couple of weeks, some of my mates have come to visit me and sit by my bedside with long faces. Soon it has been only Barry every few evenings. The small island hospital doctors tell me I should have a head scan and good physio, which they don't have. I don't have enough money or decent insurance to be transferred to the modern private hospital on the mainland. I don't know how and when my old uncle, my only relative in Wales, was contacted. Maybe Barry found him in my address book. It has taken him and his old mates at Whitehall in London another two months to lobby with the Thai consulate to arrange my transfer home by air ambulance to the Cardiff stroke unit.

****

Dusty and I are both glad to leave the house. Walking across the familiar narrow lane from the house, we exchange greetings without real feelings, with few neighbours returning home after their evening walks.

Shouting and insults thrown at the door are fading now as I let my two-year-old Alsatian off his chain. He sniffs around me for a few moments before dashing to the other side of the field. Behind me, over the bridge and the low hills, the already set sun still throws some colours at a few high clouds.

Soon evergreen trees become only large cones and balls of darkness. New leaves in the others are still holding on to some of the brightness from the day. As I gently walk towards the bench by the stream, a chattering couple pushing a pram cross hurriedly. Memories flood back of happy family walks through the same path, which used to take away all my niggles of the day.

A black and white puppy runs towards me. It smells my boot and looks up as if asking, 'where is the other one?' An old brown Labrador gives up chasing the puppy and waits to rest its tired hips.

Sitting on the empty bench, I try to forget everything and enjoy the dark canvas above being filled with faint stars one by one. The stream in front is now only layers of murk. My dog is still somewhere by the trees, now just clumps of black.

It's time to go home soon to read a bedtime story to my daughter before she goes to sleep, the only thing I can look forward to for the rest of the evening.

I shout out for my dog, that runs back to me. It's getting quite gloomy now, and it will be difficult to spot any dog poo on the path. Reluctantly Dusty and I make our way back home.

****

Following years of lifeless marriage, a year after my only daughter had suddenly passed away, the acrimonious divorce had made up my mind. I was not a loner but never had too many genuine friends. My parents had gone before they should have, one from a heart attack and the other from a massive stroke. In my late thirties, with no ties and trying to forget the pain of losing my daughter, a chance to follow my dreams of being involved in water sports in a warm sunny country came as a gift from the sky. It had not taken me long to make up my mind. I had vowed never to return to the UK.

After years of trying to find the right weather and surfing in cold waters in the south of England, breaking waves and diving in beautiful sunny Western Australia was like paradise. Two years later, I was also lucky to be hooked up with a ravishing Italian girlfriend doing a year's stint of holiday cum water sports in the country. Apart from the hot sex, the most fun we had together was her trying to teach me her grandma's perfect sauce. Toned bodies of ours often substituted plates to taste her cooled-down sauces. Then, after she went back to Italy, a few months down the line, I had found the perfect place to come and work as a diving instructor on this popular small Thai island. No regular girlfriend yet, but life could not be better.

****

Weeks of scans, physio, speech therapy, occupational therapy, and whatnot in Cardiff before I was moved to my local hospital. I have had assessments, bloody assessments, one after another by different teams. For weeks I have stopped doing anything they asked me to do.

'What's the point,' I have repeated stubbornly.

A few months later, I have heard the news that my eighty-odd-year-old uncle had died from his cancer, leaving me some money in his will. The persistence of the hospital rehab team and probably the antidepressants have got me going again. Belly full of drugs daily and everything else the hospital could offer has brought me to the best that I will ever be, my doctors have said. Thanks to the NHS, I can now swallow my food, albeit slowly, can speak with a bit of a slur, and move about in my electric wheelchair. My vision is blurred at the edge on the right. Reading a book is impossible, but I can just about manage to watch sports on TV. My team Tottenham has been doing rather well lately. My left arm and leg are unyielding and limp, except when they go into uncontrollable spasms.

'Proper physio in the first few weeks would have prevented this. Let's hope the muscle relaxant drugs and the regular physio work a bit,' they tell me.

Social services have done their best to find me a place in this care home. Almost a year after my stroke, I had moved to this place, which I know will probably be my final address. I am probably the most able-bodied among the fifteen residents here.

'Did you say Coffee or tea, Rog, Luv?' Angie asks in her wonderful, almost sexy voice standing next to the tea trolley.

Watching her smile and then staring at my wasted left forearm with the limp Thai dragon tattoo, the symbol of wisdom and longevity, I say, 'can you make the bed first, please? I think it got very wet.'

One billion people worldwide live with some form of disability, making up around 15% of the global population, the vast majority living in developing countries. In the UK, over 10 million people have a limiting long-term illness, impairment, or disability - over 18 % of the population.

Disabled people do not choose their disability. Instead, it comes upon them as an accident of birth, genetics, after diseases or accidents, natural disasters, and conflicts.

Despite being 'the world's biggest minority,' people with disabilities are often forgotten and often discriminated against. They have and continue to contribute their own ways to humankind and often have interesting stories to share.

The climber
Nepal

'Ma aba jām̐daichu,' shouted Chetan to his eight months pregnant wife Dipika, who was weeding around in the small patch of potato field on the slope next to their house.

'Oh, you are leaving already. Wait for me. I will be with you in a minute,' replied Dipika.

Their second son, three years old, named Pemba, meaning born on a Saturday, came running from the field and immediately wanted to climb on Chetan's shoulder.

'Wash your dirty hands first,' shouted Dipika, coming back.

Chetan picked up his son on his shoulder anyway while Dipika went inside their two-bedroom house with a tin roof, the best one in their small village. As Chetan played with Pemba, his wife called them inside the house. In the corner of one of the rooms was the place for their prayers. A photographic image of Durga on the wall was heavily anointed with the sandalwood paste Chandan and covered with garlands. After praying together in front of the image for a few minutes, Dipika put a tilak of the Chandan paste on Chetan's forehead with the fourth finger of her right hand.

Then she picked up the white silk scarf in front of the image and put it around his neck. Next, very quietly, she said, 'Kṛpayā dhērai sāvadhāna rahanuhōs - please be careful.'

'I will and will be back in about two weeks. I would have to be here before this one comes along,' said Chetan as he looked towards his wife's swollen belly. 'Tell Sonam from me to stay around you more when he returns from school,' he shouted from outside the door.

Pemba came running outside to give him another hug.

'Go inside now and stay with Ma,' said Chetan as he kissed his son's red cheek.

Chetan walked steadily down the hill and soon reached Namche Bazar. After a quick chat at the office, he left for Lukla, only 14 km downhill.

After two sons, Dipika wanted to have a daughter. Secretly, Chetan also wanted the same, but he often told his wife that a girl's life was hard here. Maybe once we can move to Kathmandu in a couple of years. At 41 years of age, he was glad that he was now a group leader Sherpa and did not have to do more arduous work during the treks with the tourists. But it also meant he had to go to Kathmandu to meet the foreign tourists and bring them to the Khumbu area for their expeditions and treks. This also meant flying out and returning to Lukla airport, said to be the most dangerous airport in the world. Chetan hated flying and always felt more secure with his feet on the ground. Arriving in Phakding, he went for a quick visit to one of his elderly relatives who had not been well for a while.

Soon he left for Lukla, only over an hour away. Suddenly, his last night's memory came to his mind. He now felt terrible for giving out to his wife for the dal being cold. He promised himself that he must remember to buy Dipika a Pashmina in the Thane district while in Kathmandu.

Arriving in Lukla, he had a lunch of dal bhaat before collecting his flight tickets. As the small twelve-seater took off, Chetan closed his eyes and said his prayers to goddess Kali. But he could not stop thinking about the crash here of another flight only three months back, killing all the passengers and the crew. Soon, the engine roared, and the small plane ran for a short distance before flying over the rock face. It then floated for a while in the air, adjusting to the prevailing wind. Chetan opened his eyes.

Kathmandu airport was as crowded as ever; from there, travel to his office was even worse. Chetan loved Kathmandu when he first came to the city almost fifteen years back. But now, with the traffic and the pollution, it was a different place altogether. Still, he hoped to move his family here soon. Life will be easier here for all than on the mountain, and more importantly, their children would have a chance for better education like going to college. They will then be able to find safer jobs than a Sherpa, maybe working in one of those offices. He has already been negotiating with a few friends for a small place. He hoped to open a shop in the city selling Nepalese souvenirs to tourists.

'Bīsa rupaiyām,' said the Tuk Tuk assistant, breaking his reverie as the vehicle stopped near his office. After paying twenty rupees, Chetan got off, thinking that things were already getting more expensive here. It used to be only ten rupees last year.

In the head office, he learnt that there would be nine trekkers for the Everest Base Camp trek instead of ten. The tenth one has twisted an ankle on a hiking practice in the UK. Chetan and his colleague Norbu from Pokhara collected the welcome banner. They then got into the company minibus waiting outside to take them to the international airport. At the airport, the large message board showed that the flight from London had been delayed by only one and a half hours. The two Sherpas sat in the arrival lounge for a cup of sweet tea that tasted awful. While they chatted, the announcement came about the landing of the London flight. Leisurely they got up and went next to the baggage collection area, holding up their banner.

After a while, one by one, the trekkers gathered around. Chetan felt jealous of Norbu, who talked to them in fluent English, while he could only say, 'Welcome to Nepal.'

Soon all the trekkers with their luggage were loaded in the large minibus on their way to the Raddison Hotel in the city. After helping with the checking in of the sleepy-eyed travellers, Chetan found a Tuk Tuk to the house of one of his friends, where he would stay for a couple of nights.

The following day, he was glad that he did not have to accompany the trekkers on the sightseeing tour in the city. Instead, he went with his friend to check out the two places he had in his mind to rent for starting a shop, hopefully within the year. The first place near Durbar Square would be ideal, but it was a bit pricy for him. The other one near the Boudhanath Temple complex was cheaper and with more space but probably less frequented by the tourists. It also had an added advantage. There was a place within only a mile to rent for his family to stay with one bedroom, a large sitting room cum kitchen and a bathroom – perfect.

In the afternoon, in the head office, Chetan collected all the necessary papers before discussing the logistical arrangement for the next eleven days of the trek. Later, Chetan went to meet another friend, Gyan, in the city and talked about the challenges of moving his family to Kathmandu. This friend from another rural part of Nepal had moved his family here only three years back. Chetan learnt that they were still struggling to adjust to this busy city.

Gyan's wife brought plates of dal, bhaat and tarkari for the two and quietly said, 'I wish now that we hadn't moved. No one has time here for anyone. And with its filthy air, our three-year-old daughter has now developed asthma.'

After only a cup of tea in the morning, Chetan arrived by Raddison. Then, in a nearby small shop, he quickly ate Chatamari, a rice flatbread with eggs and vegetables and another cup of tea. By the time he went inside Raddison, the foreign trekkers had finished their breakfast. All of them were already down and ready to leave except one couple. Soon they too arrived, and all of them left for the smaller crowded airport.

When the flight took off with all eleven of them and flew outside Kathmandu valley, on the north, Chetan pointed out to the trekkers the twin peaks of Gouri Shankar. This sacred peak suddenly reminded him that he had forgotten to buy the Pashmina he wanted to bring for Dipika as a surprise. It has to be during his next visit to Kathmandu in just over two weeks when he will be back to collect the next group of trekkers.

Arriving at Lukla, while the trekkers excitedly talked about and took pictures of this dangerous airport at 9,334 ft, Chetan and Norbu arranged to make sure all the pieces of luggage were collected. Then a short walk to a hotel next to their office in the small town. Here an early lunch was arranged for the trekkers. Meanwhile, Chetan with Norbu sorted out all the materials for their nine-day trip - tents, sleeping mats, cooking pots, food, and all the pieces of baggage. They were then evenly distributed on the backs of Ghopkyos, a mixed breed of cows and yaks. Then, as the animals with their handlers left, the excited trekkers gathered for their first day's walk. Only fresh Himalayan air from now on, no smelly fumes from any cars in the Solo-Khumbu region.

After three hours of an easy trek, reaching Phakding, Chetan ensured the sleeping arrangements at the small hut booked for their overnight stay. While the trekkers walked around the place and to the Dudhkoshi riverside to stretch their legs, Chetan went to check on his sick relative in the village. He looked much worse, gasping for breath, and was unlikely to survive more than a few days. Chetan sat quietly with his tearful auntie for a while but had to leave soon as he needed to make sure the dinner for the trekking group was properly made. As he walked out of the house, he almost knew that he may never see his uncle anymore.

The following day was an early start, crossing the suspension bridge on the river and then a steady trek. Chetan took the tourists to a Buddhist temple by the roadside, where they excitedly turned the prayer wheels for good luck.

'You want to turn the wheels clockwise for good luck. That is the direction in which the mantras are written and the movement of the sun across the sky,' Norbu said to the foreigners.

During the next hour of walking, some trekkers were already showing signs of tiring and were glad to have a stop for lunch. Leaving Norbu to look after them, Chetan went to sort out permits for the foreigners at the Sagarmatha National Park office.

Banks of the Imjatse River were now full of flowering Rhododendrons. The tourists clicked excitedly at the high narrow suspension bridge they would soon cross. Then, with excitement written on their faces, they slowly walked on the bridge on wooden planks held together by steel wires. After reaching the other end, while the trekkers talked about the Indiana Jones film with a similar bridge, Chetan asked them to look north. Floating clouds had cleared. For a brief few minutes, they had their first view of Mt Everest.

Chetan and Norbu knew the next few hours would be the most challenging part of the trek for the tourists so far. Norbu agreed to stay behind the slowest trekker, and Chetan walked in the front. As expected, all the trekkers needed several stops on the way. Still, everyone perked up after coming out of the jungle path when they could see Namche Bazar in front, only a mile away. By the time all the nine foreigners had reached their night's stay and their dinner was organised, it was too late for Chetan to go to his village. It had to wait until the next day. The tourists would rest and acclimatise in Namche for two days.

After sorting out the breakfasts for the trekkers, Norbu was left in charge of two other Sherpas from the local area who had joined them there. Only then was Chetan free to leave for his village. First, he bought some chocolate goodies for the children and a Kasaudi, a thick brass, aluminium cooking pot for Dipika.

On the outskirts of the town, some stone cutters were shaping stone slabs with hand tools. Chetan remembered his father, whose main job was building the roads. He also worked as a stone cutter to supplement his income. Even today, these cutters don't earn more than a hundred rupees, just over a dollar, after a whole day's work. He felt lucky to have his late father pushing him to start working as a porter with expedition teams, leading him gradually over the next few years to become a Sherpa. Chetan had been beyond Everest Camp 4 several times, helping the climbers on the Hilary Steps. He had been on the Everest summit only twice – but that was a few years back. He was glad that he no longer had to make treks above the Base Camp involving the risk of avalanches on the Khumbu Icefall.

As he approached his village, his oldest son Sonam came running towards him, giving him a hug. Soon they were joined by Pemba, who said, 'Ma did not get up from bed this morning.

Chetan worriedly looked towards Sonam, who said, 'Ma was not feeling well last night either. I made breakfast for all of us this morning.'

Hurriedly they got into their house and found Dipika sitting on the bed. She explained to Chetan that yesterday while bending to weed in their field in the afternoon, she had felt a pain in her back and could hardly move and had to stay in bed. Luckily, Sonam was back from his school by then. He had been a good big boy and had put her to bed and finished their cooking.

'I am feeling a bit better now,' she said but winced with pain, trying to get up.

Asking her to say in bed, Chetan searched his bag for the painkillers he carried for the altitude headaches the tourists suffered. After giving a couple of them to her, he said, 'you stay in bed today. I don't have to leave until tomorrow afternoon.'

Chetan then gave the sweets to the children and showed the Kasaudi to his wife. Then he went in front of the images of goddess Durga and thanked that it was only back pain, nothing to do with her pregnancy. If there was any problem with that, the nearest place was the health centre before Lukla, a day's walk.

While Dipika stayed in bed, Chetan, with the help of Sonam, who had no school as it was a Sunday, finished the weeding of the field. Pemba kept running in and out of the house and tried to help them.

By the following morning, Dipika was feeling a lot better and insisted that Sonam go to his school in Khumjung, only one hour up and down the hills. Then, in the late afternoon, having cooked dinner for his wife and sons, Chetan was ready to leave. He made Dipika promise that she would be extra careful until he returned after his tour in about two weeks.

'Leave the field and weeding alone. And ask Sonam to pick up anything heavy.'

'Chintā nalinuhōs, ma āmākō hēracāha garchu - Don't worry, I look after Ma,' said Pemba, making both smile.

The following morning at Namche, the trekkers were ready very early and bursting with excitement. After night stops each at Thangboche and then at Dingboche, Chetan, with the other Sherpas, took the tourists for an acclimatisation climb to the top of nearby Nangkartshang mountain. All but one of them made it and were thrilled. On the next trek to Gorakshep, they stopped by memorials on boulders of climbers who had died attempting Everest. One of them was for a Sherpa, who had been killed in an avalanche coming down from Everest during Chetan's first expedition trek as a porter nearly twenty years back. Chetan remembered this twenty-eight-year-old Sherpa from a village across the hills from his own got married only a month before the expedition.

From Gorakshep, the following day, the other Sherpas took five trekkers to Kalapathar for their trek and first close-up view of Everest. Chetan led the four others on an easier acclimatisation trail on the Khumbu Glacier moraine. While he chatted to the excited tourists, he could not stop thinking about Dipika, hoping she did not do anything silly while he was away. He was now more determined to start a small business in Kathmandu where he could be around his family every day.

In the early morning, the whole team left for the Everest Base camp – a lifetime dream of many. Chetan led the front group, and after reaching the base camp, he left Norbu with the trekkers for a while. He went to visit an expedition team attempting to climb Everest. He met some Sherpa friends, relaxing and sitting on a boulder in the sunshine. This time somehow, he did not feel the envy he had felt before that they were going up the mountain. Although it brings more money, the time is coming soon to give up these adventures and settle with the family – Chetan thought to himself.

Later he rounded up all the trekkers to go back to Gorakshep before it got dark. Buzz of excited chatter carried on the next two days' trek back to Namche. Unfortunately, arriving at Namche in the early evening and leaving early for Lukla the following day, there was no time for Chetan to quickly visit his family. Instead, he gave some money to a shop assistant in a nearby gift shop, who came not far from his village. Chetan asked him to pay a visit to Dipika when he went home next for one night in the middle of the week.

'Buy some properly washed lentils from Hari's shop to take with you,' he said.

Back in Kathmandu with the trekkers, he took them to celebrate at the Rum Doodle Restaurant. Everyone was happy and had many photographs taken. Chetan had the morning off the next day while the tourists went souvenir shopping before their flight in the evening. He would then be collecting another batch of trekkers at the airport. He went back to Gyan's shop and asked him for more details about how he managed to buy the shop and his apartment.

'I have now decided we will move over here once the new baby is a few months old. So please try looking out for me anything suitable that comes up,' Chetan said.

Then in an old and reputed clothes store, he bought a red Pashmina for Dipika and from a street vendor two baseball caps, the type young ones liked these days.

The full quota of ten new trekkers arrived at the airport. One of them said, 'Namaste,' in perfect Hindi. Later, Chetan learnt that he was a doctor born in India and now lived in England. As before, on the previous trips, after the Kathmandu sightseeing tour, they left for Lukla the day after.

On the trek from Lukla to Namche, Chetan learnt from the doctor that he had done some mountaineering in his younger days. But he has never been to the Everest Base Camp, one of his lifetime dreams. Now in his early sixties, he wanted to fulfil that dream. Once the porters learned there was a doctor in the team, they came at the end of each day for some medical advice, most for headaches and backaches. The doctor distributed painkillers generously to them.

Before arriving at Namche, Chetan timidly asked him if he would be able to come to his village and check on his pregnant wife.

The doctor said, 'I will be delighted to, and it will give me some acclimatisation too.'

The following morning, while the rest of the team relaxed in Namche, Chetan left with the doctor after breakfast.

Once they reached his village, from the house, Pemba came running and shouting, 'Baba, Baba,' but soon stopped seeing a stranger with him. Dipika, outside their house in her Kurta Suruwal, lowered her head.

Soon Dipika made traditional Po cha, Tibetan butter tea, for them. The doctor loved it. Soon he examined Dipika. After checking her swollen belly with his hand, he listened carefully with his tube and smiled. Then he checked her blood pressure with a small machine in his bag and said to them, 'she is fine, and the baby is fine too.' Next, he took some vitamin and iron pills from his bag, instructing her to take one daily.

Outside their house by then was a big gathering of people. The news that a doctor was in the village had spread fast. No one in the villages around had ever seen a doctor.

While Dipika made dal bhaat tarkari ready for lunch, the doctor ran an impromptu clinic. A few of the older people had chronic lung problems, one man in his thirties with one paralysed leg from polio. But other patients, luckily, were of aches and pains only. The doctor sympathetically advised everyone the best he could but could not give away medicine for all. As they were finishing lunch, Sonam returned from his half-day in school. Once he also had lunch, the doctor asked Chetan to stay with his family for the day and got ready to return to Namche with Sonam.

'I will see you tomorrow,' he said to Chetan and then said, 'Bhāgyalē sātha di'ōs – good luck,' to Dipika.

Dipika came out of the door with her new red Pashmina around her head and said, 'Dhanyabaad,' with folded hands to the doctor. Scores of people lined the street as the doctor left with Sonam. More people were coming from nearby villages to see a doctor, but they were too late.

The trek was challenging for the tourists over the next few days but routine. The doctor was thrilled when they reached the base camp and had a picture taken of him with Chetan against the

Khumbu icefall. Then, returning to Namche, after thanking the doctor many times while the group left for Lukla, Chetan was glad that now he was going home. With the upcoming monsoon season, there were no more tours for a few months until late August.

A few weeks later, the monsoon arrived. It was heavier than they could remember. Chetan and Dipika felt lucky that, while some of their neighbour's houses in the village were heavily damaged in the torrents of water coming down the hills, theirs did not suffer. Only their vegetable garden was entirely ruined.

Two weeks after this, Dipika went into labour. Unlike the prevalent tradition of arranging the animal shed for her to give birth, Chetan, as on two previous occasions, prepared the smaller of their two rooms for her delivery. He made sure that all the windows were closed and used dark-coloured clothes so that the room was completely dark as per custom. This was where the mother with her newborn would spend a week afterwards. During their second son's birth, Chetan had gone against the usual practice of the mother spending alone with the baby for four weeks. Dipika had spent only a week there by herself with the newborn.

The aji, an elderly lady from the next village who had helped most of the women around this area during delivery, came and helped Dipika during her labour. To their delight, a baby girl was born without any problem, only after five hours.

Neither Chetan nor the boys were allowed to see the baby until the aji performed 'machu bu benkyu' on the 8th day. As per tradition, Chetan brought unsalted food for Dipika every day and then salted it later for themselves and the aji. The aji said both the mother and the baby were doing well. On the eighth day, for the first time since giving birth, Dipika could have a wash, comb her hair and look in a mirror. She was glowing and could not take the smile on her face.

Soon, with some of his relatives from the nearby villages present, the aji bathed the baby in plain water and massaged her with mustard oil before wrapping her in a clean old scrap of Dipika's sari. The aji then performed 'machu bu benkyu,' the baby's first rite to receive the blessings of Chwaasa Ajima, the Goddess of childbirth. The baby's eyes were outlined with gajal (soot from an oil lamp and butter), and the forehead was marked with a black tika. Only then could Chetan, his relatives, and Sonam briefly hold the baby for the first time. Gyan kept giggling as he touched the baby's hand, and she almost grabbed his.

'Have you thought about her name yet?' asked the aji looking towards Chetan.

"Yes. We want to call her Chaarumathi," said Dipika as she looked toward Chetan.

'She is beautiful and going to be intelligent – Chaarumathi,' he said smiling.

In late August, Chetan returned to Kathmandu to collect a fresh batch of trekkers. On the group's city tour day, he met with his old friend and finalised his offer for a small place for his new shop. Then he went to a few areas to inquire about finding their new home in the city. He decided to leave the final decision until he returned in two weeks. He wanted to discuss this with Dipika in a bit more detail first.

Back home after a few days, both were delighted when Sonam brought his lower secondary report. They soon agreed that the house in the Gorkha district of the city nearer to the school would be the one they would choose. Chetan and Dipika decided that the family would move once the trekking season finished in a few months, with the beginning of the winter.

In early December, the family moved to the capital with Chaarumathi, now almost five months old. Sonam was admitted to a school in the next few months, and Chetan started his souvenir shop. Chetan asked his old tour company in early April for a one-off assignment to take a group of trekkers to Everest Base camp. Back in Namche, on the acclimatisation day for the trekkers, he returned to his village and finalised the sale of his family home and land with great sadness. But he needed the money, they had accumulated debts, and his shop was not yet making any profit.

Slowly, the shop started making a small profit with the beginning of the tourist season. Chetan was busy from early morning to the late evening, trying to buy cheap wherever he could and then sell at a bigger margin to the tourists. He regretted that he now had very little time to spend with his family. Mostly he missed Chaarumathi growing up. By the time he got home, she and Gyan were fast asleep. Hardly there was any time to spend with them before he left in the morning either.

'It will get better. I think I would be able to employ a shop assistant in a couple of years,' he said during his late dinner.

Dipika nodded and did not want to say that she had been unhappy for a while after the initial excitement of their move to Kathmandu. She missed her home in their village and secretly wished they had not sold their family home and had the option of returning one day soon.

At the beginning of another new year, Gyan was admitted to a primary school. In winter, with hardly any tourists in the city, Chetan closed his shop for one day midweek every week and had more time with his children. He thoroughly loved playing with Chaarumathi, who was now walking while holding his hand. Dipika and Chetan regretted that they could hardly go out of their small one-bedroom house with their daughter. The streets were always so busy with traffic and people.

By the following March, the tourists were returning, and Chetan returned to opening his shop every day. Before the base camp trekking season began, he went a couple of times to the tour office near Raddison to learn more about the opportunity to return to his former job. However, he got the impression that they now considered him too old to be the trek tour leader. He learnt that he would have to compromise. He was asked to return in a few weeks when the manager, who was now away to a foreign land promoting their business, was back.

On 25th April 2015, Chetan arrived at the tour office by 11 am. After waiting only half an hour, he was called to the manager's office. He was greeted warmly by the manager, who remembered him very well. During their discussion, the manager said they needed someone younger as the trek leader. But then he added to Chetan's surprise that the trekking business was expanding. The company was thinking of making their Namche office bigger and needed a manager there with local experience.

'You are the person I had in mind. But I know that now you have moved to Kathmandu with the family,' he said.

Chetan tried to hide his excitement and calmly said, 'would you mind if I came back with an answer tomorrow? I want to talk to my wife first.'

As he stood up to leave, suddenly, he felt a tremor, like just before a massive oncoming avalanche on the slopes of Everest above Camp one. The pictures of trekking teams on the wall shook violently before falling to the ground and shattering to pieces. Then, within a split second, the whole building shook fiercely, and all of them in the room were swinging like pendulums. They were on the ground floor but felt like the three-storey concrete building was collapsing above them. The windows of their room shattered. Part of the ceiling from their room fell to the floor. Chetan ran out of the building with the others to the street through a broken window. In front of him, the city had been turned into rubble of collapsed buildings and upturned cars. Completely disoriented, people were running in panic in all directions.

Chetan felt almost dizzy but wanted to get to his family as soon as possible. He tried to run, but the grounds trembled again fiercely. He fell to the ground, and a piece of broken glass from the window of the nearby building came flying and shattered over him. Ignoring the small cuts on his face and hands, he got up and ran again. There were squeals and screams from people trapped under concrete slabs, rubbles, upturned cars and everything else. How he wished they could have afforded to buy those mobile phones for themselves to talk to his wife still a few kilometres away in their house.

As he ran, the ground shook every 15- 20 minutes destroying even more of the city, as if it was not already enough. The three kilometres run to their house felt like almost a lifetime. Chetan had to go through a narrow lane about a hundred metres before their dwelling. The buildings on either side were in a sorry state and still collapsing, with their balconies and walls scattering on the lane.

By the time he managed to reach the middle of the lane through the falling debris, he could see the building with his family's small flat on the first floor was now a complete mangle of bricks at a distance. Then, as he started running towards the catastrophe, Sonam came running towards him from the other direction, covered with cuts and bruises.

Choking with tears, he somehow managed to say that the earthquake had started while he was at his school. Luckily their classroom was next to the playfield, and most children had managed to escape through the broken windows. But their teacher and some children had died from the falling roof. Sonam had run to their house to find that it was gone. He sobbed violently.

Holding Sonam close, Chetan tried to run toward what was once their house. But with another even more violent aftershock, the building next to them crashed mightily over them, killing them instantly.

In 2015 April and May, an earthquake of 7.8 magnitudes in Nepal killed nearly 9,000 people and injured more than 22,000. More than 600,000 homes were destroyed, and over 288,000 were damaged in the 14 worst-hit districts.

Farmers lost livestock, crops, tools, and irrigation works. More than half of the country's schools were damaged and destroyed, and close to 1 million children (one in three) were out of school. Many of the already sparse health centres and hospitals were ruined, as were water and sanitation systems.

The coffee pot

The jet-black ornament with its slender handle and an elegant long snout sits proudly on the windowsill in sunny Devon. Made of clay with an elongated yet exquisite neck, it looks exotic. The little ring of cushion it sits on is made of grass which has been coloured in a few different shades.

'Oh, this is beautiful. What is it?' Not for the first time, it has caught the eyes of many coming for a cup of coffee or dinner at my place.

'It's an Ethiopian traditional coffee pot,' I have often said in a well-pleased tone.

In a busy marketplace in Dilla sits a middle-aged woman on a dirty plastic sheet with rugged holes spread over the ground. She looks thin, almost emaciated. She is wearing a blouse, once probably colourful, but now just covered with grime with a few buttons missing in the front, revealing her shrivelled-up breasts. Her long skirt is equally dirty and is now of indeterminate colour. Her sandals, made of tough rubber, lie next to her. But her beautifully braided hair is what catches my eye. In front of her is spread a variety of clay pots.

I ask my friend Nenko about the small pot with a long delicate neck.

He explains that this is a miniature traditional Ethiopian coffee pot. 'But it is too small to use even for one person, only for the tourists. The bigger ones at the back are the ones we use. They are called Jebena.'

'What's her name? Where has she come from?' I ask.

My friend talks to her for a while in Amharic. Then he turns to me and says her name is Meti. She has come to Dilla from her village about twelve kilometres away on the back of a horse cart with a few other women.

I ask, 'how many does she hope to sell today?'

Nenko talks to her again and says they don't usually make this size pots. Her husband makes all the clay pots with the help of their children, and she brings them to sell once a week. Nenko explains that she comes to the Dilla market only once a week because she has also to look after her family, children and animals. She has heard that more and more 'firingis' are coming to Dilla these days. Apparently, they like to buy something small to take home as a souvenir.

'How much does she make in a week?' I ask.

Nenko speaks to her for a while and then translates that she can make about four to five hundred birrs on a good week. But much less in the winter season between June and October when there are hardly any firingis. The bigger pots sell for 15-20 birrs. The smaller ones are more difficult to make.

'How much does she want for this one?' I ask.

Nenko says 20 birrs. I give her 25 birrs, a whole pound, and thank her.

Meti smiles through her missing front teeth and says, 'amasheganalu.'

When we return after looking around the market, the place is almost empty under the hot midday sun. Meti has covered up her merchandise with a dirty rag. Under the shed of the branches of the solitary eucalyptus tree over her stall, she was unpacking her lunch - some injera and wot.

As on the next day, Sunday, we have no training programme at Dilla Hospital, I ask Nenko, 'could you please find out if we could visit her village tomorrow?'

Nenko talks to her, and I watch her smile and nod. She will be home tomorrow.

The following morning, three of us from the visiting team leave with Nenko and the driver Sulaiman. As we leave Dilla town and drive on an orangy unpaved rural road, we see scores of people wearing white, walking and holding their children's hands.

'They are going for the Sunday morning prayer at the church,' says Nenko.

After driving for another kilometre or so, we hear a loud chorus of singing from a distance. Nenko asks the driver to stop, and we get off our car. Outside a tin-roof building, some young children stop playing and gather around us with wonders in their eyes while Nenko speaks to some adults. They welcome us inside the building bursting with songs from nearly a hundred men and women in their Sunday whites. We sit in the back row and watch near the front row, several people standing and rhythmically dancing while everybody sings. Pure joy and ecstasy in the face of everyone.

After watching this for nearly twenty minutes, we leave quietly. Outside, the children gather again and ask for a pen. We find a few pens we had with us and give them. I ask one of the 7-8 years old to write her name on my notebook. She does so proudly. Then I ask another boy to do some adding-up maths.

While everyone looks on, he does correctly, '8+14= 22.'

'Gobezi bet'ami gobezi nehi - brilliant, you are very clever,' I say, and his eyes light up with pride.

The children wave at us with smiley faces, and we drive again.

On the road, we pass two ladies walking towards the town, bent with the weight of dry eucalyptus branches on their backs. Behind them, a young girl of no more than ten is also carrying tree branches on her back and trying to keep up with the older women. Seeing our car, she stops and gives us a wave with a smile on her lovely face drenched with sweat. From a distance, we see children carrying on their backs and upon their heads big plastic cans with water going towards their villages. We soon see several long queues next to a deep water well pump by the roadside in another couple of kilometres. Women and children are waiting with large jerry cans to fill up with the trickling but clean water.

Soon the road becomes hilly, with coffee bushes on the hill slopes and beautiful flowering jacaranda trees. Nenko reminds us that the low hills of Yirgacheffe, which we will be visiting next week, produced the best quality coffee in the world. But its farmers do not get enough support and publicity compared to the big corporations in Brazil or Columbia. They hardly make a living despite the hard labour.

Then we approach a small settlement of mud huts.

'These are the only type of houses we have seen outside the towns since we left Addis. What are they called?' asks one of us.

'They are called tukuls. In Ethiopia, over 80% live in villages, and people live in the tukuls, the only type of house everywhere. Only some government buildings and banks have brick buildings,' replies Nenko.

Sulaiman says something in Amharic, and Nenko translates, 'but the rich people in the villages sometimes have tin roofs on their tukuls.'

Almost all the tukuls have some coffee bushes around them and some beautiful flowering plants on their grounds.

'Those are Calla lily flowers. It is Ethiopia's national flower. They are one of the oldest species of flowers known to mankind,' says Nenko proudly.

Branches of green to red olive-like coffee seeds hang from the trees. Once ripe red, they would be harvested and dried in the sun.

'How much coffee do they get from each bush?' asks one of my colleagues.

Nenko answers about 20-25 kilos per bush. Then he continues, 'do you know that the first-ever coffee in the world originated in the Simien Mountains in the north of Ethiopia? Legend says goat herders noticed animals became energetic after eating the berries from a particular kind of bush. Herders then made hot drinks with these berries to find it had kept them up and fresh all night. That's how coffee drinks came to the world!'

Our four-wheeler stops outside a cluster of tukuls. Even before we get off the car, the children gather around shouting, 'Firingi. Firingi.'

Some of the younger ones hold our hands as we walk towards the tukuls over the fields. Nenko makes some enquiries, and soon we were outside one of the tukuls. The walls of the tukuls are made of mud, and the roof with eucalyptus branches.

A young mother stands by the door with a baby on her lap. Two small children hung by her, and soon the coffee pot seller lady appears from inside with a smile and invites us in. By the door, we notice eucalyptus branches on the floor with some bright petals of lily flowers thrown over.

'This is to welcome you and also to keep out the dust,' says Nenko.

The tukul had an outer wall, and within this, they kept their animals.

'We have five cows and two bulls. We don't have horses or donkeys like my neighbours,' says Meti as we walk behind her.

Inside another wall lived her family of seven – her husband, his father, and her widowed sister with her three children. We learn Meti had four children. Two of them died very young. Her son now works in Awassa in a hotel, and her seventeen-year-old daughter died last year from heavy bleeding during her first childbirth. Meti's first grandchild, the newborn, had also passed away a day later.

Inside, the tukul is very dark. I ask permission to take some pictures inside with my flash. Meti nods. To my surprise, a picture of David Beckham was hanging on one wall! We all laugh and learn her son is a mad football fan! As our eyes get adjusted to the darkness inside, we notice a faint glow at the other end. There is an open fire for cooking by the wall. No wonder so many children end up with burns in Ethiopian villages! Next to the fire on a bed on the floor lies an elderly man.

I say, 'Selami,' to him.

He tries to get up and starts coughing. We learn he has been unwell for nearly six months and is now even unable to leave the hut.

As we get ready to leave, Meti says something to Nenko.

'She wants you to stay for the coffee ceremony. It is traditional for all first-time visitors to the house in Ethiopia to be treated to a coffee ceremony. Even in the poorest homes in the villages.'

We immediately say, 'it will be our honour.'

Soon Meti's husband arrives from the field and says, 'Selami' to us. Next to the door around the eucalyptus branches, he lay out several low three-legged wooden stools. We sit on them in a circle around a small charcoal stove. Meti comes dressed in a white robe. Sitting on another stool, she roasts dried coffee beans on a hot plate. The aroma of the roasting coffee is intoxicating. Then, she uses a heavy wooden bowl called mukecha and a wooden pestle called zenezena to crush the beans to coarse ground.

Next, in a small black Jebena, but bigger than the one I bought from her, she boils water with a straw lid on the pot over a small charcoal fire. Then she puts the ground coffee in the boiling water after removing the straw lid. While waiting and watching all this with intrigue, we all get served with popcorn, totally unexpected! By then, the water is boiling over the pot, and Meti removes it from the heat. A tray of very small cups without handles is arranged with the cups close together next to her. Meti pours the coffee in a single stream from about a foot above the cups, filling each cup equally without breaking the stream of coffee.

'Doing this way, the dregs of the coffee remain in the pot, stopping coarse grounds from ending up in the coffee cups,' says Nenko as we watch with wonder.

We drink the coffee, which is extremely bitter and thick, sticking to my palate. I take sips of water from my bottle to clean up the sticky coffee in my mouth. While I think to myself, all this fuss just for a tiny cup of coffee, Meti pours more water into the same pot for boiling. We get another round of popcorn served around. Once the coffee pot starts boiling over, a second round is served - less thick but still very, very strong. Soon she put more water into the coffee pot, and we get the third round. This time a bit lighter but stronger than any coffee I had tasted in Italy. After these three rounds of coffee, I did not sleep for three nights!

After a while, we say, 'amasheganalu' and have to leave. The children now hold our hands and laugh all the way to our car.

Snow flurry outside my house this afternoon. I look at the black coffee pot on my windowsill, and after a while, I take out a dusting cloth. I dust the shiny pot with loving care and then put it back on its colourful ring cushion.

Ethiopia, the birthplace of the human species, is also considered the birthplace of the coffee plant and coffee culture from as long ago as the ninth century. The coffee ceremony is the most important social occasion, even in the poorest houses. Being invited to a coffee ceremony is a sign of respect and friendship

In the UK, we drink daily approximately 95 million cups of coffee. While the global coffee market of around $102 billion is clearly profitable for food companies, it's a very different story for coffee farmers. Coffee growers receive only 1-3 % of the price of a cup of coffee sold in a café. Also, 70% of coffee farm labour is provided by women, who receive 40% less than their male counterparts. Fairtrade was started in response to the dire struggles of Mexican coffee farmers in the late 1980s. As a leader in the global movement to make trade fair, Fairtrade supports and challenges businesses and governments, connecting small-scale farmers with the people who buy their products. In 2020, the country with the largest market for Fairtrade-certified products was the UK. Although 82% of UK consumers care about Fairtrade, only 25% of coffee sold in the UK is Fairtrade (only around 5% in the USA)!

Coffee farming is further compromised by the impacts of the climate crisis, increasing the risks farmers face depending on coffee sales.

It's my husband's fault – I have told him off

Awassa. Ethiopia 2015

At the end of the first long day of advanced skills training in emergency surgery and obstetrics in Awassa in southern Ethiopia, Murida Shamil approached me timidly. She was 28 years old and had travelled nearly a day and a half by public transport from her rural primary hospital near the Somalia border to Awassa to attend this course.

'Dr Biku, I am sorry I have been late each time during breaks to return for the training, and you all had to wait.'

I said, 'no problem. What is the matter?'

'It's my husband's fault. Sorry. I have to breastfeed my 6-month-old daughter. He was supposed to bring the baby in between breaks. I have told him off now,' she said.

When this advanced skills training programme circular reached Murida's primary hospital, she had jumped at the opportunity. The hospital authority had promptly agreed, as this would give their only surgeon, serving a population of nearly two million, a chance to widen her skills. It has not taken much for Murida to persuade her husband to come along with their young baby. As one of the only four teachers in the local high school of eight hundred children, he was glad to have a chance to have a break and spend some time in the regional town as a guest of his uncle with Murida and the baby. It will also be the first time his uncle and aunty will see their baby daughter Enguday.

At dinner, I reflected with Aberra and Yifru on the last few years of our work together. It all started in 2000. Aberra, a surgeon and Yifru, a gynaecologist, our local link coordinators based in

Awassa, worked tirelessly to develop the link's programmes. In its first years, our Wales-based health link had gradually expanded basic skills training to the non-doctor health officers and nurses of all of the southernmost region of Ethiopia, SNNPR, with a population of nearly sixteen million people.

In 2006 we were at Arbaminch, near the country's southwestern tip, for one of our skills training weeks. Many had come travelling for up to two days to attend the programme.

On the first morning of training there, one health officer came to me and said, 'Hello, Dr Biku. Do you remember me?'

His face looked familiar, and I said, 'I remember your face but remind me.'

His name was Wodajo. He had attended our second training programme in Awassa. When I asked what he was doing these days, he replied he was working in a remote hospital close to the Sudan border. Like many in the region, he said his hospital had no doctor, only another health officer. To my surprise, he said he was doing caesarean sections and laparotomies for emergencies. When I asked where he learnt to do these operations because we never taught about doing major surgery in our skills courses.

Wodajo replied, 'you taught us some skills and gave us confidence. I used them plus improvised. The next hospital with a surgeon is more than 150km away on a poor road. Patients would not survive if I sent them there.'

This got me and Aberra thinking. If this was possible with only basic skills training, how many more lives could be saved with a structured training programme? Fortunately, we managed to arrange a meeting in Addis with the Health Ministry on our way back through Aberra's contacts and our link's reputation.

Back in Addis, in an all-day meeting arranged by the health ministry, the surgeons from Addis University and the WHO Ethiopian representatives were also invited. I, with Aberra, outlined our idea for a formalised training programme in emergency surgery for the non-doctor health officers and senior nurses to save lives in rural hospitals. While all others agreed, Addis surgeons objected, saying these health officers and nurses were not doctors. They could not agree to such a programme.

The health ministry asked politely but sternly which of them would like to be posted in a rural hospital. The city-based surgeons backed out immediately. I had never come across forming a national task force within a day! But it happened there by the end of the day!

In the next two years, led by Yifru, a formal three-year Masters' programme, Integrated Emergency Surgery and Obstetrics (IESO) training of the health officers and nurses, started in the country.

Yifru, Aberra and I proudly explained to the rest of the trainers at our dinner table that after our initiation, this Masters' programme for the IESOs was rolled out in Ethiopia in 2009. It was the first such programme in the world to train non-doctor health workers in all aspects of emergency surgery. Yifru elaborated that since then, this MSc programme has expanded to 11 universities in the country. The first batch of graduates qualified in 2012/13. By the end of 2015, there were over 800 trained IESOs in Ethiopia. The training programme hoped to have one IESO available per

100,000 population throughout the country. Many rural hospitals currently only have IESOs carrying out emergency operations. Even in the regional hospitals, they played a significant role. Everyone at the table raised their glasses to the IESOs. While the other IESOs were at the dinner, Murida could not attend as she was putting her baby to sleep in their relative's home.

Murida herself had successfully trained for three years initially as a health officer. At the age of 22 years, she was then working as in charge of a health centre serving a population of more than eighty thousand. Soon she had the opportunity to join the IESO Master's programme after a tough entrance exam. While doing her Master's, she also got married.

All the trainers, most from the UK, were impressed by the skills of these IESOs attending the course, easily comparable to the level of a trained registrar back home. We had asked the attending IESO to bring their logbook of operations since graduation. In our advanced skills training course, twenty-four IESOs attended most travelling long distances. Together, in about three years, they had already carried out about 5000 caesarean sections, operated on over 500 ruptured uteruses, and done 1300 laparotomies for various other emergencies. Thus, potentially saving almost 7000 lives. Additionally, they had saved 5000 newborn lives in the past three years alone.

Yifru, Aberra and I could not hold back our proud smiles, thinking about the breathtaking impact on the whole country by these IESOs. We knew they would continue to save hundreds of thousands of lives in Ethiopia for years to come.

Murida told us at lunchtime the next day that she graduated as an IESO only three years back. Since then, she has done 400 successful caesarean sections. She had also dealt with 64 ruptured uteruses (with only one death) and done approximately 200 laparotomies. Thus, saving over a thousand lives already. And within that time, she also managed to have her first baby daughter!

She said almost in a joking voice, 'in the later stage of my pregnancy, I was praying every day that I don't end up needing a caesarean section myself. I knew apart from me, there was no one else to do CS within 100 miles. Luckily, all went smoothly.' She smiled, stroking her daughter's hair.

It had been a routine for us to stroll at night after dinner in the street towards Lake Awassa, empty by then of traffic and people. The most refreshing way to unwind after a long day of work.

On the last night, after the end of our week-long programme, we walked towards Lake Awassa. Hardly anyone on the road. We noticed from a distance a small family on the footpath under one lamppost. We saw a mother with a baby fast asleep on the pavement as we came near. Next to them, a girl of 7-8 years was reading a book. Then, as we stood beside them, the mother woke up. We asked what the little girl was reading. The child gave me her notebook, her homework for English for the next day at school.

This hunger for knowledge of the young girl living on a footpath was the best lesson and memory to treasure for me of my 16 years in the country.

In 2017, our article, 'Saving lives by task sharing: The role of the non-doctor surgeons,' was published in the African Journal of Midwifery and Women's Health. This study clearly demonstrated that these non-doctor surgeons saved thousands of lives of mothers, newborns, and others every month in Ethiopia. In addition, an audit of their performance quality showed that they were easily comparable to those of medically qualified surgeons in other countries.

Choice

Banjul, The Gambia

Ali's favourite team in the EPL, the Reds, Liverpool FC, have already conceded a goal in the first twenty minutes. Like a few other staff at the big resort hotel in Banjul, the capital of The Gambia, Ali was glued to the large latest high-definition screen in the massive front lobby by the reception desk. Only half an hour back, he had collected a group of tourists from the airport in the hotel minibus. He had then helped the hotel staff bring the guests' luggage to their luxury cabins by the pools. Ali's ten-hour shift finishes in fifteen minutes, the same time as the halftime break of the match.

The Reds score a beautiful goal from fifteen yards outside the penalty area. 1-1 now. Three minutes of extra time to play before halftime. Ali looks up at the wall clock – 8 pm. His shift is over. Ali drags himself out of the hotel and walks towards his home, only two miles away.

After the street with the luxurious hotels on the Atlantic shore, he is soon on the dark, broken road between shanty houses with choked-up drains next to them. Ali, in his mid-thirties, is still thinking of his playing days at the top club in the city only a few years back. As a midfielder, he was often called Steven Gerard, the famous midfielder of the Reds. Once, he had even caught the attention of a scout from a European club. He had continued to play regularly, even after he was married. But it was becoming a struggle with his new job as a driver at the resort.

Ali's parents died when he was very young, and he was brought up by an uncle and aunt who were childless. He had met Khalima at the market where she worked with her mother in one of the shops selling vegetables and fruits. While Ali was buying some fresh okra and bell pepper, the pretty young woman commented to the nearby seller that she had seen this man's picture in the newspaper.

Ali had fallen head over heels at her beautiful smile.

They had a few outings, six-foot-tall athletic Ali and a very pretty but only five-foot tall Khalima. He had sent kola nut to her as greetings and a declaration of his marriage proposal only six months later. When Khalima had accepted, Ali's uncle, with one of his male cousins, had gone to meet her family. While the elders talked to agree to decide the dowry, Ali had discussed football with Khalima's only younger brother outside the house. The young boy has seen him playing in the town league. To him, Ali was a hero. After some complicated negotiation, 1500 Dalasi (28 US Dollars) was agreed upon, almost two months' salary Ali earned at the time as the hotel's restaurant kitchen staff. But despite Ali's insistence, his uncle and aunt had paid for breaking the kola nuts and the wedding costs, which were several times more. Two weeks later, in the local Mosque, after speeches and prayer, 'Takka', tying the knot, had taken place.

With Ali's regular earnings at the resort and Khalima bringing in a small amount working in the market, they have managed to rent a small one-bedroom apartment in the city. It was almost three miles from Ali's workplace, but anything closer to the resort area was beyond them. After a blissful six months, Ali was over the moon when Khalima declared she was pregnant. He had stopped playing in the league and had taken on extra duty at the hotel as a porter so that Khalima could work less and less at the market. When their son was born a few months later, they named him Omar. Khalima had stopped working in the market. Ali had worked harder, only wishing they lived a bit closer to the resort so that he could spend more time with the mother and the baby.

Within ten months, Khalima had become pregnant again. As Ali had hoped secretly, this time it was a girl. They had named her Fatoumata, which soon became Fatou. Both the children had grown happy and healthy. At the age of four, they had managed to get Omar into Albaraca Nursery School in Sukuta, thanks to one of the assistant hotel managers, whose sister ran the place. His charm as a brilliant footballer has not escaped the hotel management team. As the nursery school was nearer to his resort, now Ali had a chance to drop his son at the school on his way to work while Khalima and Fatou picked him up later in the day. To pay the small fee and other expenses at the school, Ali had taken more overtime work on most days of the week.

Soon after talking to the hotel manager, Ali found that they were looking for more drivers for their fleet of minibuses. Ali had spent his sparse spare time trying to get his driving license which meant even less time with his family. But he had managed to get his license within a few months. Soon, Ali was working as a driver at the hotel. This had given him a small but significant pay rise for which he was extremely grateful. Then Fatou also joined the nursery school, allowing Khalima a few hours to earn some money at the market stall.

But Khalima was pregnant again and had a difficult pregnancy compared to the last two. By the time they had their third child, a son, Momodou, it was time to decide on the proper schooling for Omar. They had chosen a primary school rather than sending him to the Islamic School in the nearby Mosque so that he could learn some English, which would give him a better career prospect in the future.

Unfortunately, the school was not without costs. Although they did not have to pay any tuition fees, even in the first year, the cost of buying Omar's school uniform, books and supplies added to almost 1000 Dalasi. And Khalima was now full-time looking after her new baby and two other children. Even with Ali's slightly better pay, it has been a struggle for the family.

A year later, when the time came to send his daughter Fatou to primary school, colleagues in his resort, many in a similar position, had asked Ali to forget the idea. Many had their children either not going at all or dropping out of school. And she was a girl, after all. What good will it do to her as she will be married in a few years and starting her family anyway? However, Ali had gone against all of this and Fatou was also admitted to the primary school. Secretly Khalima had been proud of this decision. Managing the money for his family was now more than a struggle.

His aunty had then suddenly passed away at the age of only sixty-one. Ali would have liked to bring his seventy-year-old uncle to their house to look after him. But their one-bedroomed place was already crowded with three children and themselves. As his uncle worked as a fisherman in his working days, there was no question of any pension. Without hesitation, Ali and Khalima had agreed to support him with money and everything else in his own house. Now Ali hardly had any spare moment, but luckily Khalima had managed to find a job bead making for one of the local souvenir shops. Omar and Fatou found it fun helping their mum assemble the colourful beads in chains. It hardly paid anything, but any money was desperately welcome.

By the time **Momodou** was four, there was no way they could send him to nursery school without taking out one of their older children from the school. It was a hard decision, but Ali and Khalima agreed to keep **Momodou** at home until he was seven. They had hoped that by then, things would improve for them, and he would be able to go to primary school. But Khalima was pregnant again. Soon another baby boy was born, whom they had named Hassan in memory of Ali's uncle, who had died only the week before his birth.

Although Fatou was always happy going to school, lately, Omar had been reluctant to go. He was using every excuse to miss school. After this had been going on for a few months, one day, Ali took him to a football match in the city. They got the best free seat with his old club reputation. After the game, Ali found out why Omar had been avoiding school lately on the way home. Two teachers in his school often beat the children with sticks if they made the slightest mistake. In Omar's class alone, five children out of forty-five had already dropped out because of this.

Ali had visited the headteacher at school, who had joined only a few months back. He had listened to Ali and promised he would look into it soon. After this, Omar was happier going to school, especially when he was included in the school's junior football team. Whenever Ali could get away from his work early, his best moments were taking Omar, Fatou and Momodou to the small field next to the Mosque to play football until dark. Although very young, Ali could easily see that Momodou had talent in the game.

By the time Momodou was seven, their landlord had evicted the family after only three months' notice. He was going to turn the place into a modern apartment block. After a desperate search, they found another single-bedroom flat in the nearby part of the town. It had slightly more space in the larger living room cum kitchen area but was more expensive. Money was now really tight for them, and regretfully they had to decide not to enter Momodou into a school. Momodou was also happy not to have to go to school and played all day with the other dropout children in the area. Ali knew that several employees at work, especially those in lower-paid jobs like security guards, either could not afford to send some of their children to school or had taken them out after only a few years. But it was no consolation for him.

Luckily, within a year, the hotel manager had called him to his office to say that the resort would expand by building several more cabins as more tourists were coming to The Gambia. The management was thinking of creating a post of transport manager, and they had Ali in mind. This will give him more money although more responsibility and possibly some extra hours at work.

At home, Khalima and Omar and Fatou have been teaching Momodu to read and write and basic adding up plus subtraction. He had picked up on those quickly and could read a little but was more interested in playing football.

When Hassan was four, Ali was already the transport manager and bringing in more money. Despite the cost of schooling for Omar and Fatou increasing with their growing years, Hassan was soon admitted to the nursery school. This stretched their budget to the limit. Momodou, now nine years old, had already missed out on nursery education and then the first few years of primary education and was no longer fit to start school. Momodou had taken up a job with almost no pay helping in the vegetable market, where Khalima had started going again while Hassan was at the nursery.

Ali, on his occasional few hours off in the afternoon, looked forward to playing football with his children in the local park whenever he could get away. Nine-year-old Momodu was already taller than Fatou and almost as tall as Omar. In Ali's experienced eyes, he could see Momodu's talent in the game, reminding him of his younger days. Omar had less time for football as he was now busy preparing for his Basic Education Certificate Exam (BECE) so that he could attend a Senior Secondary School. He wanted to be a doctor.

Fatou was getting busier with her studies too, and had less time for football, although she played for the school's girls' football team. But her primary sport was athletics, and she had already won several medals at interschool competitions in short-distance running. She wanted to be a teacher. When Momodu was ten, Ali had arranged for him to join his old football club's junior team. Momodu had excelled. Within a year, he was playing for the under 14 team, in the same midfield position where Ali played.

The assistant manager at the resort had another proposal for Ali. Their only child, a daughter who was now almost twenty years old, was still unmarried. After finishing high school, she had been to college but had given it up only after a year. Her parents were getting worried as she was not getting any younger. The assistant manager had known Ali for many years. Admired by many, Ali was known to have a strong character. He had proposed that he would be delighted if Ali was interested in taking their daughter as his second wife. His family would bear all the cost of breaking the kola. They already had an apartment in the city earmarked for their daughter as her wedding gift.

Later Ali walked home in the late afternoon. On the streets near the resort, by now, at the end of the tourist season in late May, vendors were trying to sell souvenirs for the last few days before closing their shops for the next five months in the rainy season. Ali knew well that these vendors, at best, made a profit of 1000-1500 Dalasi per month, equivalent to 18-25 dollars, the same price as a single buffet dinner at the resort hotel where he worked. A young pregnant mother sat outside her stall of colourful clothes and beads. It did not look like she had made any sales today. But she was trying to stay happy for the moment by nodding to the tune of Taylor Swift coming from a nearby coffee shop. The last of the wealthy tourists were bartering for a bargain to save a few hundred Dalasi in the next shop.

Outside their house, Omar, Fatou, Momodou and Hassan were playing football with the new football Ali had bought for Momodou's birthday only the week before. The children all begged him to join. And Khalima soon came out with their new six-month-old baby girl Aminata, named after his auntie, on her lap with a smile.

Ali's mind was made up.

The Gambia is among the least developed countries, ranked 175th on the world's human development index. Over 95% of the population is Muslim. In The Gambia, contraception is a major contentious issue because of its socio-cultural and religious dimensions. It is used by only 10-20% of women. Polygamy is a common cultural and Islamic practice. The dropout *rate for primary education in The* Gambia *is about one in four.*

The RAF pilot

London suburb, England. 2000

'Mr Rawat?' called Ashok, opening his cubicle door. An eighty-year-old turbaned Sikh gentleman came through, walking ramrod-straight and wearing an RAF tie. After he sat down, Ashok asked about his problem.

'The last couple of weeks, I have been feeling dizzy when I get up, and sometimes I also feel quite lightheaded. So, I thought I'd better get it checked out.'

After asking a few more questions, Ashok checked his blood pressure and said, 'your blood pressure is quite high, Mr Rawat. When was the last time you saw anyone?'

'I don't think I have seen a doctor since I broke my leg during the war,' he replied.

'Well, your pressure is very high. I am going to start you on some medicine, and we will check again in two weeks.'

Before leaving, Mr Rawat asked, 'Doctor, you look like an Indian. I was born in India too. Where are you from?'

'I was born in Nairobi but grew up in Calcutta,' replied Ashok.

'My uncle was in Calcutta. He was stationed in Fort William.'

'Was he in the army then?'

'Yes. Listen, Doctor, I can see the surgery is teeming with people now. I will see you in two weeks, and maybe then we will have more time to talk,' said Mr Rawat as he walked towards the receptionist.

Ashok learned more about Mr Rawat during his next few visits to his surgery. Anil Rawat was born in 1920 near Dehradun in North India. His father served in the district magistrate's office in the town as a clerk. The only son of his parents, Anil, went to college in Delhi after finishing school. His father, a loyal servant of the British, wanted him to become a lawyer and go to England to train as a barrister. However, while in Delhi, Anil got the taste of flying and joined the local flying club. After six months, he got his Indian commercial pilot licence and a job as a pilot with a local airline.

Only six months later, the war broke out in Europe. Anil was immediately interested when he found an advertisement asking pilots to join the Royal Air Force. He went to his father in Dehradun the next day and asked his permission.

'This is an opportunity for me to serve the Raj in their time of need, and also, I can fly to many places in the world.'

While his mother cried, his father, always a faithful servant of the Raj, agreed with his son.

Anil and only twenty or so other Indian pilots were accepted and started their training as commissioned officers of the Royal Air Force. He felt proud to be amongst the elite band of pilots in India. Chacha Singh, older than him by only eleven years, was already known worldwide for his solo flight from England to India and narrowly missing out on the Aga Khan Prize. He was Anil's hero in the group. After a short training period in India, the group travelled by boat to England. As officers of the Royal Air Force, all were eligible to travel first-class with individual cabins.

A Sikh RAF officer in wartime England was a rare sight. People were always respectful of an RAF officer. In the evenings, cinema halls and restaurants did not want money from them. Often people saluted Mr Rawat and called him, 'Sir.'

'You know what impressed me most? Despite all the carnage during the Blitz, the intense German bombing campaign, the British people showed no panic. They were really courageous.'

Stationed near Croydon, Anil was chosen to fly fighter aircraft in the Royal Air Force.

'Within the first year, a quarter of our Indian pilots were killed,' Anil said.

After flying several sorties during the war, Anil's plane was hit by enemy fire on his way back from France after escorting a bomber. He just about managed to fly his damaged plane to the English shore but broke his left leg after jumping off with a parachute. By the time he was discharged from the hospital, the war was over.

By this time, his father had retired, and his mother was seriously ill with kala-azar in India. He returned to India, and after India became independent, he joined the Indian Air Force. His father, unfortunately, soon passed away from a stroke. His mother also died within a year. Anil got married three years later. His wife, Kapila, was sadly diagnosed with blood cancer only a year after their marriage. Despite the best treatment, she died four years later.

'When I retired in 1975, I wanted to settle down somewhere I could be comfortable. To me, in India, even if you have servants, everyday life is a struggle. Nothing goes smoothly. There is no discipline or order. I had fond memories of England during the war. I had no one close in India. So, I decided to come to live in Great Britain.'

Anil was allowed to enter the UK in the same year as the Government's 'honoured guest.'

'When I first arrived, the local people generally didn't like us, coloured people. Once, I remember being confronted by a white neighbour living in the same street as me. He was telling me, 'you coloured lots are good for nothing. You come over here and take our jobs, and we don't like you.'

I told him it was my country, too, and I had fought for it. If we had been late in getting to the battlefront, this country would have been in the hands of the Germans. I told him not to give me trouble as I had sacrificed a lot for this country. The man apologised to me, saying he didn't know.

'These days, many people here see an Indian with a turban and assume he does not understand or speak English. So often, I had to ignore rude comments behind me from people who thought I did not understand what they were saying.'

'This is modern England. They are supposed to pretend they don't notice certain things, such as whites and Asians or blacks,' replied Ashok.

Mr Rawat added, with some sadness, 'do you know, public servants like bus drivers or even police constables in the street will be rude to me or almost ignore me? And then, in the next minute, they would be polite and helpful to old white people much younger than me? During the war, I would have been called 'Sir' by their grandfathers!'

His blood pressure was now under better control. Ashok advised him to continue with the medicines and make an appointment to be seen again in six months unless there was a problem.

Ashok saw Mr Rawat again about five months later. He was returning to his car after a house call in the neighbourhood in the afternoon. As he was walking on the pavement, he noticed Mr Rawat was attending to his small flower bed in front of his house.

'Hello, Mr Rawat. I did not know this was your house,' said Ashok, standing by the fence.

'Hello, Doctor. So nice to see you. Please come in for a cup of tea,' said Mr Rawat, opening the front gate.

Ashok had no more house calls that afternoon, and his surgery was not due to start for another hour and a half. He said, 'thank you, that will be nice,' before following him into the house.

The small living room was neat and tidy. There was a framed picture of the Queen over the fireplace. A photo of Mr Rawat with his wife at an earlier age hung on one of the walls. There were also a couple of pictures of himself with his squadron in front of a Spitfire fighter on the other walls. After bringing a pot of tea, milk, sugar, two cups, and some plain biscuits on a plate, Mr Rawat sat next to Ashok.

'You must have enjoyed the fiftieth-anniversary celebration of VE Day at the cenotaph. And you will be now looking forward to the sixtieth anniversary in a few years?' asked Ashok, sipping his tea.

Not looking directly towards Ashok, Mr Rawat replied in a forlorn voice, 'I have never been invited to any of these official celebrations.' Then he added, 'I have privately gone to the cenotaph many times and laid flowers in the memory of my fallen comrades. I wrote to the Ministry of Defence asking why I was not invited to the fiftieth-anniversary celebration. No one has replied—so far.'

Ashok looked at him, genuinely shocked, and said, 'are you serious?'

Mr Rawat nodded sadly.

After a few more minutes of conversation, Ashok said, 'It was great talking to you. I learned a lot. But I must go now, Mr Rawat. Thank you very much for inviting me. Hopefully, we will see each other again soon.'

In the next few months, Ashok had a few more visits to Mr Rawat's house and many interesting chats with him.

Mr Rawat said one day, 'people here now forget the truth. Did you know that in the Second World War, the British Indian Army, which was a volunteer army, was the largest volunteer army in history? Two and a half million fought in the war for the British, fighting on three continents in Africa, Europe, and Asia. Eighty-seven thousand Indian servicemen lost their lives, another thirty-five thousand were wounded, and over sixty-seven thousand became prisoners of war. All the cotton parachutes used for dropping supplies in the Eastern Front in Burma, over four million of them, were produced in India.'

Then he added, 'they were awarded about four thousand decorations, including thirty-one getting either the Victoria Cross or the George Cross. Field Marshal Claude Auchinleck, the commander-in-chief of the Indian Army, said that the British 'couldn't have come through both wars if they hadn't had the Indian Army.' Even the British Prime Minister, Winston Churchill, paid tribute to 'the unsurpassed bravery of Indian soldiers and officers.'

Ashok replied, 'I also know from history that up to two and a half million died in India due to the war-related famine and diseases at the time. In 1943, a major famine in Bengal led to millions of deaths by starvation. Churchill declined to provide emergency food relief.'

Ashok continued, 'this was when the Indian National Congress demanded independence before it would help Britain and London refused. During the 'Quit India' campaign in August 1942, tens of thousands of its leaders were imprisoned by the British for the duration of the war.'

As Mr Rawat poured more tea into their cups, he said with sadness, 'this country has changed so much now. Do you think it is getting worse,

Doctor? In the last few weeks, I had rubbish pushed through my letterbox. And once, someone threw a brick at the window. You can see it's still cracked. I hope you don't face this kind of racial prejudice in your work.'

He went on to say, 'the British National Party are now using the Spitfire as a symbol of their party. They forget that people from different backgrounds helped in the Second World War. I am proof of this—I was flying a Spitfire!'

The next time Ashok saw Mr Rawat was in his surgery three months later. He had to attend the A&E a week earlier with an injury to his face. Mr Rawat now needed his stitches removed and checked in the GP surgery after.

Apparently, he was out for his usual evening walk across the park from his house. He did not know, but a BNP rally had finished in the town only an hour earlier. A small group of supporters were going back home through the park when they found this elderly man with a turban taking a stroll. After throwing verbal abuses, one pushed him to the ground before the rest started kicking him. Fortunately, people in the park had come to his rescue and called for an ambulance. Ashok found Mr Rawat still shaken from the incident.

'This is not the England I remember,' he said before leaving.

Ashok came across Mr Rawat for the very last time when he had to attend his house on an out-of-hours call. Apparently, he had been having mild pain in his chest since lunchtime. He did not feel well enough to come to the surgery and was not keen to unnecessarily call for an ambulance. When Ashok arrived at his house, Mr Rawat was barely conscious and appeared to have had a massive heart attack. Ashok had called for an ambulance immediately.

Before the ambulance arrived, Anil Rawat, the RAF pilot, passed away in front of Ashok in his beloved England.

An Indian volunteer RAF pilot Mahinder Singh Pujji, awarded the Distinguished Flying Cross for outstanding bravery and service to Britain in WW2, was treated as a hero in wartime Britain. At 90 years of age, he talked about his disgust at the lack of recognition given to the role of blacks and Asians fighting the war. 'Everyone loved me, and I fell in love with England. That was the mistake I made.' What offended him most was how Indian servicemen's role during WW2 was afterwards completely forgotten. 'Officially, I don't receive any invitation to Remembrance Day services. They don't know I'm here.'

A new permanent exhibition called Diversity in the Royal Air Force was since opened in 2009 at the Royal Air Force Museum Cosford in Shropshire in the presence of Squadron Leader Mahinder Singh Pujji. Following Pujji's death at 92, his statue was erected in Gravesend, Kent, in 2010.

The Queen

Northern Territory. Australia 2013

After a mind-bending visit to Ubirr, with its Stone age art from at least 30,000 BCE to the present, we arrived by the East Alligator River. Then a boat ride on the river in the pristine wilderness of the world heritage landscape. Next, we disembarked on the Arnhem Land side of the river. Sitting in the shade of large paperbark trees, then enjoying Top End's famous barramundi for lunch.

At the Bowali Visitor Centre, our guide was a young woman in her late twenties. She provided insight into the Aboriginal culture and local mythology. She tried to teach us to throw spears and boomerangs in an open area next to the visitor centre. Although she threw with natural ease, we all failed miserably, even after several attempts. Soon she led us into the jungle nearby and taught us a few bush survival skills. She showed how to find the right plant and fruits to eat and dodge crocs while in the water for swimming or collecting water.

Afterwards, sitting by the visitor Centre, the young woman told us more about the vast lands of Kakadu. She explained that these lands are now jointly managed by their Traditional Owners and the Australian Government. As seven of us sat in a semicircle around her, she demonstrated weaving baskets from the reeds. Then she asked us if we had questions for her.

I asked if she had any chance to get any education living here and did she feel isolated in this remoteness. She answered calmly she went to a boarding school in Darwin to complete her secondary education. Unfortunately, she did not enjoy the experience there at all. When someone else asked why she calmly replied it was because of subtle and overt racial discrimination.

Our driver cum guide came and said that Kakadu airport for our flight back is only fifteen minutes drive and the flight is not for another two hours. He asked if we wanted to spend more time here or go to the airport now. We all said we would like to spend more time here than at the airport lounge.

A couple from our group went outside to practice more boomerang throwing. The rest of us sat around the young woman with cups of coffee and asked her to tell us more about her growing up here.

The young woman spoke in a calm, graceful manner.

'My name is Jedda, or Djida, which means little wild goose,' she said with a broad smile. Then she said that hundreds of Aboriginal groups, diverse in language, culture, and spiritual beliefs, had lived on this continent for approximately 60,000 years. They had their political, legal, economic, and social infrastructure in place. But, then, only two hundred years back, the colonisers came, armed with the most oppressive of ways, motivated by their desire to acquire the land here to expand Mother England.

After a short period of silence, she looked at us and said, 'my father escaped being one of the Stolen Generation Aboriginal children.'

Someone asked what the stolen generation was.

Djida calmly explained the Stolen Generations (also known as Stolen Children) were the Australian Aboriginal and Torres Islander descent children removed by force from their families by the Australian government agencies and church according to their own laws. This happened mainly between 1905 and 1967, although in some places, it continued into the 1970s. Even the official government figures show that up to one in three indigenous Australian children were forcibly taken from their families and communities between 1910 and 1970.

Djida continued that her father had gone to town with his older brother, younger sister, and their mother for the day. Suddenly the place was surrounded by the police, who had rounded up four mothers with their children and put them on a bus. After only about five miles, they had stopped and pulled out all the mothers from the bus. The mothers had thrown themselves in front of the bus, wailing, but the police had pulled them away with force. Luckily, in the mellow, her father, who was only eight at the time, had managed to escape. The place was not far from where his family lived, and he had managed to find his way home. But his ten-year-old elder brother, his six-year-old sister and six other children from their community were taken away. The mothers had chased the car, running and crying while the children on the bus screamed.

From then on, the people had been extra careful and tried to avoid authority as much as possible. The families had not been able to find out about their stolen children afterwards despite going to many of the offices in the town.

Because of this, Djida's father avoided going to any school but learnt how to live off the land from his father and the elders. From the age of fourteen, he had worked as a labourer for several cattle ranches but, like his father, had refused to work in the mining sites, which paid more. Djida explained this was because most of these mining sites were destroying the Aboriginal heritage sites.

She then said, 'did you know that the indigenous people who had lived on this land for many millennia were not considered a citizen of this country until 1967? They had no access to unemployment benefits or anything else.'

Djida continued saying, many years later, the lost eldest son of the family had returned when he was twenty-three. He had been kept in a dormitory run by the missionaries. Like many, he was often beaten up for speaking his indigenous language to other children. He had cried with shame while telling his younger brother that in the dormitory, he was sexually abused by the priest. Although he had learned some English, he was trained mainly to work as an agricultural labourer. After he was discharged from the institution at sixteen years of age, he was sent as a worker on a large cattle farm, working like a slave. He had picked up the habit of drinking there, a culture alien to the Aboriginal people. But he had hardly any choice as much of his paltry wage was paid with alcohol and tobacco. The rest was with some basic food.

Looking up at us, Djida explained that Aboriginal people infrequently used only mild alcoholic drinks made from various plants before the invaders arrived. Their use, however, was strictly controlled. Aboriginal words for 'alcohol' meant 'dangerous', 'bad' or 'poisonous'. But alcohol use changed significantly after the white people arrived. Invaders paid the indigenous labourers in alcohol or tobacco, if paying at all. She added that in the earlier days, a favourite spectator sport of the white people in Sydney was to ply Aboriginal men with alcohol and encourage them to fight each other, often to the death.

Now, alcohol has devastated much of the indigenous community around the cities and towns in the country. Domestic violence, fire injuries, falls and drownings, and road and industrial accidents were rife among alcohol users. Added to that is unemployment. As a result, depression and suicide rates amongst indigenous people were very high. At the age of 26, Djida's uncle committed suicide.

'What about the stolen girls? Your father's sister?' asked someone.

'Only two girls, aged twelve, out of the five returned two years later. They had escaped together one night from their boarding school, nearly a hundred miles away. But they had managed to navigate their way back. We, Aboriginals, are nomads. Tracking a hundred-mile route is not uncommon. But my auntie was never seen again,' Djida replied. The boys and girls were kept in separate institutions in different, often faraway places. Many stolen girls were physically, emotionally, and sexually abused and sent to work as domestic servants at white men's houses.

Djida then said with pride written all over her face that her grandfather was the community elder and had fought for land rights together with other indigenous leaders for decades. He had been sent to prison many times. This became a national news headline during a protest against giving their sacred cave site lease to a Bauxite mining company. Hundreds of indigenous people were beaten up and imprisoned for several years in the 1960s.

Finally, in late 1977, almost a full year after the Aboriginal Land Rights Act was passed in the Northern Territory, her grandfather had won the rights back to his own land with others in his tribe. Unfortunately, he died only a year after. As per tradition, Djida's father had become the tribal chief – the king.

Lack of regular employment compounded by discrimination had been made worse by alcohol-related issues in the community. Djida proudly stated, 'after meeting with other tribal chiefs, my father had banned alcohol in this area for the last ten years. Some people still go to the small town and buy alcohol but are not allowed to bring it home.' Then she added now this was the same in many other tribal areas regarding alcohol.

'What about your mother?' asked someone.

A faint smile appears on her face. 'She was fearless. She was a big and strong Torres Island woman. Whenever someone said something racist to her, she'd just go and knock them flat. Once, she punched a truckie driver for calling her 'jin' behind her. Mum was strong because she'd had to fight as a black woman in this country all her life. No one messed with her.'

Then she added, 'unfortunately, she passed away when I was only nine.'

When I asked her to tell us more about her schooling, she calmly replied that she went to the local community school until she was twelve. She absolutely loved it. Someone from our group mentioned that we visited a local school on yesterday's tour in the neighbouring area. It was the only one-teacher school for the area's fifteen students from transition to grade six.

'The school enrolment varies here year to year between five to twenty-five depending on who was living in the area at the time,' replied Djida. Then she added, 'we all loved it there. Apart from the usual school stuff, we also learned bush skills.'

But after that, she was sent to a boarding school in Darwin because there was no teaching for the higher classes in the local school.

'I absolutely hated it there.'

I asked, 'why?'

Djida replied that it was not only her but all the indigenous children also hated it there. Many left soon after and never went back to school. The white boys regularly barked at the Aboriginal girls as if they were dogs. Not only the white boys and girls called them 'jin' or 'nigger,' but even some of the teachers also used those words within their earshot.

'What is jin?' asked one of our group.

Djida explained it was an offensive term used by whites in connection with the sexual exploitation of Aboriginal women. 'Many indigenous students are skipping school to avoid racism and bullying even to this day. Like many, I felt disgusted. I hated it every day and often cried,' she said.

'I stuck it out till the end of my school years and even got high marks in my final exam. But I lost any desire to go to college and to continue to suffer the abuse. It was not worth it anymore.'

Djida then elaborated that as the tribal chief here, her father is respected by everybody around. She said proudly that as his only child, Djida would become the chief one day of the tribe when he became too old. She has a 2-year-old son and was very happy in this place.

'Do you miss not living in the city with modern facilities?'

'No – not at all,' she answered. She then said, 'I have many friends here. We meet and have great fun with many ceremonies. Sometimes we go together to the towns for shopping. No, we do not miss a single bit.' Djida added, 'now I teach my two-year-old and other local children jungle skills, and when he is a bit older, he can go to the local school.'

'How many people are in your tribal area?' asked someone.

'In our own community, currently between 100-120 people live in an area covering over 2000 sq. km. But our people often move from one place to another.'

Djida proudly added, 'my father is now in his sixties. When he becomes very old or passes away, I will become the leader of our tribe here – the Queen.'

The driver returned with the other two tourists, and it was time to go to the airport.

We all thanked Djida. At the end of the hour we spent with this young lady, I was most impressed with her calm demeanour and intelligence. I truly believe she would be a great Queen for her tribe one day there.

Indigenous Australians are still fighting for their lands 30 years after the landmark Mabo v Queensland case in June 1992, notable for recognising the pre-colonial land interests of First Nations people within Australia's common law. The struggle continues for the people who have lived on the continent for 50,000 years. And while native title rights are enshrined in Australian law, they are not always upheld.

In May 2020, the international mining giant Rio Tinto made a calculated and informed decision. They drilled 382 blast holes in an area of its Brockman 4 mining lease that encompassed the ancient rock shelter formations in Western Australia's Pilbara region.
In a matter of minutes, eight million tonnes of ore were ripped from the earth. With them, 46,000 years

of cultural heritage were destroyed. The Puutu Kunti Kurrama Pinikura people, the traditional owners of that land, lost their material connection to sacred sites of ceremonial, clan and family life, the basis for their political and social organisation. For this hefty price they paid, Rio Tinto lawfully gained access to 135 million dollars of high-grade iron ore.

Also, a court decision in the early 2000s held that the rights of ranchers and farmers leasing lands in Western Australia prevailed over the native title rights of the Miriuwung and Gajerrong peoples. The court agreed with the plaintiffs that certain 'existing interests, like grazing, can extinguish' native title claims.

Sharing the grief of a loss

Lake Cargelligo. NSW

Australia. July 2013

The ambulance rang to say to be on standby. They were bringing an injured child from Lake Cargelligo.

In the small town of Griffith, over 500km inland from Sydney, people were just waking up on an early winter morning. I had arrived only a few minutes back at the hospital and was going to start my leisurely weekend ward rounds. Our operating team got ready immediately after the call.

The ambulance called again to say the patient had a cardiac arrest on the route. Luckily, they had managed to resuscitate him and should be at the hospital within the next 15 minutes.

The anaesthetist and I waited for the ambulance in the car park outside the A&E. Soon, they arrived. We took him straight to the operating room. While the anaesthetist was getting him ready and I scrubbed, we heard the story from one ambulance crew. This 14-year-old boy had stabbed himself in the stomach in the night.

Opening his abdomen, we found he has torn his vena cava, a major vessel. Despite our try and a large amount of blood transfusion, the child died on the operating table forty-five minutes later.

I went outside to speak to the family and give my condolences. I said, 'very sorry, we could not save the child.'

They thanked us in tears. The child's mother was not there. The grief of the sudden loss of my own child only a few months back and her memories flooded back.

The family told us more about the incident. This young boy's close friend, a 17-year-old cousin, had committed suicide by hanging himself only six weeks back. This 14-year-old had hardly spoken to anyone since. Then, last night he had an argument about some trivial matter with his mother before going to bed. His mother had woken up at around 4 am, probably because of motherly intuition, and had gone to his room. She had found him covered in blood and barely conscious. The mother immediately called for the ambulance. But at winter dawn, on a kangaroo-infested road, it took almost two hours for the ambulance to reach him in their place near Lake Cargelligo.

I had driven to the tiny Aboriginal settlement of Lake Cargelligo only a few weeks before this incident, only to explore the area. The two-hour drive from Griffith through the empty roads with vast fields of grazing kangaroos and emus was very relaxing. About 135 km outside Griffith, the town was by a small lake fed by the Lachlan River. The place was almost empty in mid-morning. The tiny town was once a prosperous mining area for gold, silver, copper, lead and zinc. Lake

Cargelligo and Murrin Bridge, on the other side of the river, were also once large reserve settlements of the Wiradjuri people. But the area was almost deserted since all the precious metals had been extracted and the mines closed. Now, only about a thousand people live in these two places.

Back in my place later in the day, I opened the photo albums of my first daughter. Only three months back, both of us were so much looking forward to her coming to Australia for a couple of weeks' holiday. Flights were booked. I had spoken to her only a few days before the date she was to come over. She sounded like having a heavy cold but was in good spirits. She had asked me if I needed anything to bring over from London. I had said I really did not need anything. When she insisted, I asked her to get me a decent bath pillow as I could not find one in the small town of Griffith.

Then a late-night phone call shattered my life forever. Coming back to the UK for her final arrangements, I found a note in her flat from the post office of an undelivered package. At the post office, I collected the bath pillow she had purchased online for me to bring to Australia. Now, alone in my rented bungalow in Griffith, only with her pictures in the album in front, floodgates of tears opened.

For about a year, I have already been training emergency skills for Aboriginal Health Workers in the Griffith area. Now I resolved to organise basic emergency skills training for local health workers in the Lake Cargelligo area shortly. Only two months after the sad passing of the young boy from there, I returned to Lake Cargelligo for the training schedule. I also arranged a breast awareness programme for the local women at the same time. Breast cancer in Aboriginal women was on the rise and often diagnosed late due to a lack of awareness, leading to a higher death rate.

A female Aboriginal Health Worker accompanied me from Griffith to Lake Cargelligo. On our journey, she told stories about growing up as an indigenous woman. Although she was now a graduate, it was a struggle for her all the way because of discrimination. She said that even in this second decade of the 21st century, subtle and overt discrimination against Aboriginal people was rife. High unemployment, alcohol abuse, and mental health issues leading to suicide rates were high in the Aboriginal community.

At the end of the all-day programme in Lake Cargelligo, while I was talking to the attendees, a woman came up to me.

She said, 'Doctor, thank you very much for trying to save my son.'

She then gave me a hug, and silently, we both shed tears.

Bluebell woods

Her dull eyes have lit up now.

First time in many months,

on her tired, wrinkled face

is that almost cheeky smile

we have always known

and will remember.

The winter, although mild,

has been very wet this year

and has crawled to spring.

Lately, the hospice nurses have come daily.

Syringes full of strong stuff

have kept the pain and sickness bearable.

No more visits to the hospital,

the oncologists have called time.

She has not talked about this for a while.

We have been to the garage,

all neatly arranged as before,

though everything

covered with thick cobwebs.

The dusty wheelchair

has been taken out for this day.

'Da' would have had many memories on it.

Between the ancient trees,

midmorning soft sun sends

thousands of rays to the ground

covered with still wet mosses.

Amidst the rising mist,

this vast carpet of bluebells

never before looked so magical.

For this moment,

dewdrops on their long leaves

has turned into thousands of tiny stars.

She chose to wear her faded blue cardigan.

Her slippers are tight on her swollen ankles.

Carefully we wrap

the favourite blanket over her lap

before rolling the creaky wheelchair.

In the middle of this delicate scent of blue madness

She and we, all smile now.

I have been there – I think

Ivybridge, Devon. 2019

I park on Clifton Close and ring the bell at number 24 house. Almost a full minute wait before I see a shadow slowly approaching behind the ground glass panel. After a bit of fumbling noise, the door opens.

'Good afternoon, Keith,' I say.

The blank expression on his face changes slowly. 'And you are?' asks Keith.

I tell him my name as I have done every week for over a year and say, 'we will go for a walk soon if you want.'

'Oh. Come in,' and Keith slowly walks towards the conservatory.

'Have you had lunch? Do you want a cup of tea?' I ask.

'Lunch? I don't know. I made some tea, but it tasted horrible.'

I walk to the kitchen. By the sink is a mug with a teabag in some greenish-black liquid. Next to it is a carton of orange juice. The sandwiches for lunch left by Linda, Keith's wife, who has left only a short while back for a well-deserved three-hour break, are left unwrapped.

Then I check inside the fridge, clearly labelled outside in bold 'FRIDGE.' There is no milk in there. Then I find the milk carton on the living room's coffee table.

'Why don't you have your sandwich while I make you a cup of tea? Then we will go for a walk.'

Keith slumps back in his chair as I unwrap his sandwich and bring it over on a plate. While I make his tea, he says. 'two sugars with extra milk, please.' I laugh to myself, as I have heard many times before.

He finishes the sandwiches quickly. And then drinks the tea slowly. He must have been hungry, I think to myself. After clearing the plates, I sit next to him.

On the coffee table in front of him is the AA road map of Great Britain. Keith always loves maps and pictures of places. I open the map of England and ask him to find where we are. He studies the map carefully and looks up at me. I tell him we are in Ivybridge, in the southwest. He looks at the map again and finds the place after a while.

I ask, 'do you remember where you grew up?'

'Wollaton,' he says promptly.

'Where is that?' I ask like I have done many times before.

After thinking only for a while, he says, 'I think it is near Nottingham.'

'Can you find that place on the map?' I open the detailed map page of East Midland.

He spots the place quickly and then finds Wollaton and gives a smile.

'So, you grew up in Wollaton?'

'We had our house next to a lake,' he says.

'Did you swim there?' I ask.

'Only in the summertime.'

'What did your parents do?'

'My father had tire business in another town,' he replies.

'And your mother?'

'Oh. She was busy doing housework.'

'Did you have brothers and sisters?

'Only two brothers. They called us three musketeers,' Keith grins.

'What are their names?'

I notice that each time he speaks of his growing-up days, his accent changes slightly – he goes back to his East Midland accent.

Keith thinks for a while and says, 'Alvin was the older one.' He thinks for another minute and says, 'I can't remember the younger one's name. He was very naughty. Both are dead now.'

I say sorry and ask him more about his growing up.

I notice his answers are trailing off.

'Shall we go for a walk?' I ask.

One of his knees makes a creaking sound as he gets up quickly and heads towards the door.

'Wait. Let me get your coat. It's cold and windy outside.'

I find them in the cupboard marked 'OUTDOOR COATS' in bold and help him put on his coat, woolly scarf, and hat. He tries to put on his woollen mittens.

'Do you want to use the toilet before we go?'

'Oh yes,' he says, handing over his mittens to me and going inside the toilet.

Several minutes pass, and no sound from inside.

I knock and ask, 'are you alright there, Keith?'

No answer. After knocking another time, I open the door. Keith is just standing in front of the toilet with its lid down. I lift the lid and tell him, 'there you go,' before coming outside and leaving the door half-open. I am glad that none of the doors inside the house no longer has any locks.

After a while, I hear a flushing noise and then water running as he washes his hands. He is always meticulous about washing his hands. Then, as he comes out, Keith asks, 'what are we doing now?'

'We are going for a walk,' I say, pulling up the zip of his trousers.

Keith fumbles as he slowly locks the front door before putting the keys in the breast pocket of his coat as usual. Outside, their car is on the drive. Linda often walks to the town.

Keith blurts out, 'KLM 0TV. That's my car. K for Keith, L for Linda and M for Miller, my surname.'

I ask, 'and what are T and V for?'

He replies, 'T for Thomas, my father's name. And V for Violet, my mother's name.'

Then he adds, 'do you know KLM is also the name of a plane? I used to fly in that a lot.'

I already knew from Linda that Keith was an engineer with a reputation. He worked for the central government and frequently travelled abroad for meetings and conferences.

'When did you last drive your car, Keith?'

'Only a few days back,' he replies.

But I know he has been stopped from driving over a year back because of his dementia.

'My keys?' he asks.

'In your breast pocket,' I tell him.

He taps on them and gives a satisfying smile.

We slowly walk up the path and stop by a farm. Keith loves looking at animals and starts counting the sheep.

'One, Two, Three ---, Eleven,------ Eighteen, Nineteen,' he finishes counting. I check, and it is nineteen. He is always accurate with his numbers.

'How many cows are there?'

He counts quickly and says, 'five cows and three calves.'

We walk further, Keith picking up and clearing fallen small twigs from the path all the way. He is always fussy about that.

As we go further. I ask, 'did you have animals growing up in Wollaton?'

'We had a dog.'

'What was its name?'

Keith thinks only briefly and replies, 'Mungo. It was called Mungo.'

'What kind of dog was it?'

'It was a big dog.'

We have already walked for about half an hour. I know about his osteoarthritic knee and say, 'let's go back for today.'

'Can we go a little more?' Keith asks.

'Alright. Five more minutes, then we must go back. Otherwise, your knees will play up later.'

Back outside the house, he looks at their car and proudly repeats, 'KLM – that's Keith Linda Miller. Do you know KLM is also the name of an aeroplane I used to fly?'

'When was the last time did you fly, Keith?'

Only a couple of months back, he answers.

'My keys?'

'In your breast pocket,' I say to him.

He taps on them and takes them out with a smile. His hands shake as he tries to put the keys in the lock, and I help to open the door.

After he settles down on his favourite sofa inside the house, I make him another cup of tea with two sugars and extra milk.

I ask him, 'so, you used to fly on KLM? Where did you fly to?'

'Many places,' he answers.

'Like where?'

He looks blank. I show him New York on the world map – 'yes,' he says. Berlin – 'no.' Paris – 'yes, but I have also been there on a boat.' Next to him on a table is the framed photograph I know of his son and two daughters with Keith and his wife, Linda.

Bringing over the picture, I ask, 'who are these?'

He takes the frame from me and looks at it for a long time. I point to his son and ask, who is this with you in the picture?

'I don't know, really.'

I point to his daughters and ask. He shakes his head again. Then I point to Linda, and this time he says, 'Oh, that's Linda.' He then puts his finger over his own picture and, with a smile, says, 'that's me.'

As weeks go by, I notice Keith is getting even slower than usual in his movement. Although he loves to go out for a walk, he winces with pain in his knee only after a short distance. Instead, occasionally I take him by car to the Moor, only three miles away.

On the way, he looks out of the window and says, "I used to walk up this path with my dog." I know they did not have any dogs since they moved here more than ten years back.

While we cross over a creek, he asks me to stop. I stop making sure there is no car either way on this quiet single-lane road. He wants to get out. I let him out carefully, saying that we could stay only for a minute. Even for that minute, his whole face brightens up. He picks up stones and throws them into the narrow stream like a child. Then he throws fallen dry leaves into the water and watches them float downstream.

'Let's get back into the car. Another car might be coming,' I say as I help him back into his seat.

Then as we drive slowly on the rough track, about two hundred yards below the car park, Keith points to a rusty old broken cottage. Many old apple trees with moss hanging from them are next to it. I stop briefly.

He says, 'we used to have a place like this in Wollaton. We often went there to steal apples. The lady of the house sometimes chased us with a stick. She was horrible.' He finishes with a grin on his face.

We walk up only a few yards from the car park in the Moor with a glorious view all around on a sunny day. Dartmoor ponies roam the craggy landscape with winding trails. Below are the river valleys cutting through farmlands with granite stonewalls, hedge banks, farmhouses, and many dilapidated buildings. Further away on the horizon in the south, a sliver of sea glistens.

Keith immediately starts counting the cows in a field below us.

' - Three-- Twenty-eight. Twenty-nine.'

I know he will be correct. I adjust the scarf around his neck – it is early summer, but it is pretty windy on the hill.

While we walk up the path a few more yards, I hear him singing loudly.

'Hair of gold, eyes of blue
Prettiest girl I ever knew
Skin as white as precious pearl
She was my Tipperary girl,' he sings with a big smile on his face.

'That was wonderful. So, who was your Tipperary girl, Keith?'

He only grins and repeats the lyrics.

As we have already come up almost a hundred yards from the car park, I say we better go back.

Keith hums and says, 'let's go a bit more.'

After walking up the path another few yards, I stop Keith from going further. Although only slightly downhill, I know that going down to the car park would make Keith cringe with his arthritic knees. We stop, and he looks around the hills and down below with a fresh gleam in his eyes.

I tell Linda beforehand and take Keith to the seaside only twenty miles away on another hot summer day. Then, before going out, as I open the cupboard for his coat, he picks up a heavy coat and woolly hat.

'It's a hot day today, Keith. Let's get a lighter coat. Otherwise, you will be boiling.'

I help lock the front door, and Keith puts the keys in his breast pocket as usual.

As we walk to the car, he asks, 'my keys?'

'In your breast pocket.'

He taps on them with a smile.

On the way, going over the hills, Keith hums, 'she was my Tipperary girl.'

After parking the car, we go down to the beach.

'My gloves?' he asks, checking his coat pockets.

'We left it at home. It's very sunny today.'

Keith is in top spirit seeing the waves at a distance. The sandy beach is full of people, some swimming while others are only sunbathing. The children run in and out of water, following the gentle waves crashing on the sand. Keith starts walking towards the water.

'Let's take off our shoes and leave them here, Keith,' I say.

I help him take off his shoes and leave them with mine. While I take off my socks, Keith is already walking happily towards the water with his socks on. I realise he wants to dip his toes in the water.

'Let me help to take off your socks too.' Then I roll up his trousers.

Both of us walk ankle-deep in the water. Keith's face lightens up like I have not seen before. A wave comes and splashes on us, and he giggles like a child.

Soon we walk back towards the car park.

Keith sings loudly, 'Oh, we do like to be beside the seaside.'

Children building sandcastles turn towards him and giggle, and Keith sings louder with a broad smile on his face.

Then, we sit by a café and have some ice cream.

'My gloves?' he asks again, checking his coat pockets.

'We left it at home. It's very sunny today,' I repeat.

Afterwards, as we walk towards the car, he hums, 'we do like to be beside the seaside,' and carries on the same tune all the way back.

On a sunny day, I arrive at 24 Clifton Close to find a note left by Linda. The small whiteboard, along with other daily instructions, says Keith had not slept all night. Best to spend time with him at home. I go into the small back garden and pull out the easy chairs for Keith and me. After he settles down on a chair, I look around at the flowering plants.

I point to the single rose bush of dark red flowers with velvety petals and say to Keith, 'this rose is beautiful.'

He gets up slowly from his chair and comes across. 'I think I planted this one,' he says.

'They smell wonderful,' I add, taking a sniff.

Keith puts his nose right next to one of the roses. After sniffing for a while, he says, 'I cannot smell anything.' Then he asks, slightly agitated, 'What is this flower called ?'

'It is a rose.'

'Oh.' He looks at the flower for a minute and asks, 'what is it again?'

'Rose,' I repeat.

He loses interest and slumps back in his chair. I go to the kitchen to make ourselves some tea.

'Extra milk and two sugars for me, please,' Keith shouts.

We make a few more short visits to the Moor in the summer sunshine in the next few months.

'I used to come here often when I was a child,' Keith says.

I know he did not grow up around here. I ask, 'when did you last come here, Keith?'

'Oh. Many, many years back, when I was a child,' he replies before starting to count the animals on the fields below.

Each time after counting the animals, he happily sings,

'Hair of gold, eyes of blue
Prettiest girl I ever knew
Skin as white as precious pearl
She was my Tipperary girl.'

Another time I take him by car to the nearby riverside for a walk there. By the stream, he picks up a flat piece of stone and skims it over the water. The stone bounces a few times over the water before it sinks. He tries it again with another piece, and it disappears after only one bounce. Slightly frustrated, he picks up another one, and this time, it bounces several times on the water. Keith glows with pride.

'You are very good at this,' I say to him.

'We used to do this in the lake behind our house. Alvin was not very good, but Kevin was a champion.'

'Who are they?'

'Oh. They were my brothers. Alvin was the older one, and Kevin was younger than me. They used to call us three musketeers. Kelvin was the naughty one. Both are dead now.'

I say, 'very sorry.'

Returning to the car, I ask, 'Did you enjoy skimming the stones on the water?'

'What?' he asks.

'You were throwing the stones on the water to bounce like a frog just now.'

'Don't know what you are talking about.'

'Skimming stones on the water like a frog. In the river behind those trees.'

'What river?'

'You were skimming flat stones on the water there like an expert.'

He replies, 'no. The last time I skimmed stones on the water was with my brothers when I was young. We used to do this in the lake behind our house. Alvin was not very good, but Kevin was a champion. Both are dead now.'

I say, 'very sorry.'

In the next few months, although Keith perks up each time with the Moor view and hums his favourite song, I notice him slowing down rapidly. Going even 20-30 yards from the car park gradually becomes a struggle for him, and we return only after a brief stop.

Soon, I find his trousers wet on a few occasions, and I help him change into clean ones with difficulty. But Keith's interest in maps and places remains as strong.

While having tea, I show him the names of places around the globe on world maps.

'New York? – I have been there, I think,' he says. 'Sydney? – Yes, I think so. Berlin? – I don't think so. Brussels? – Yes, I went there often. Paris? – yes. Toronto? – no, I don't think so. Rome? – yes, a few times.'

Sometimes, I bring my iPad and show him pictures of places. Keith always brightens up. Looking at some places like Sydney, Rome, and Washington DC, he says, 'I have been there, I think.' While some other places like Melbourne, Mosco, and Prague hold no interest for him.

I ask him, 'Keith, what do you miss most about not being able to remember?'

He thinks only briefly and replies, 'places I used to travel.'

Going up the Moor becomes less of an option as autumn approaches. Even going outside of their house for a short walk stops soon. Keith is sleepier than ever.

We spend more time looking at maps and talking about his growing up in Wollaton, which always brightens him. Seeing the world map and photos of cities he had visited on the iPad makes him talk with excitement. At other times, he falls asleep as we are talking. At times he cannot even remember who Linda is.

I buy a card for Keith and bring it over during my next visit to wish him a happy 82nd birthday. When I press the bell at the door, Linda appears.

'Our daughter Sally and one of our granddaughters, Mia, came over from Reading a couple of days back for his birthday tomorrow,' she says.

'Then, I will wish Keith happy birthday and leave you alone with him for today.'

'No, no. Would you mind staying with him for an extra hour, please? Three of us are going out to do some shopping.'

'Sure,' I say as I go in.

Linda introduces me to her daughter and says, 'he is a voluntary community care worker.'

Keith is on his usual sofa, half asleep. His ten-year-old granddaughter is sitting next to him, drawing a picture. I say hello to them and then wish Keith a happy birthday the next day. He wakes up and just smiles. I praise Mia for her drawing.

She asks me, 'how old are you?'

'Only seventy-four, a youngster like you,' I reply, making her chuckle.

Linda soon leaves with the other two.

I say to Keith, 'it must be lovely for you to see your daughter and granddaughter after a while.'

With a vague look on his face, he asks, 'who?'

I repeat, but he does not seem sure what I am talking about.

'Your daughter Sally and granddaughter Mia, who came over for your birthday. They were sitting with you just now?'

'Don't know what you are talking about. Shall we go out for a walk? It is sunny outside.'

I get him ready and make sure he uses the toilet before going outside. Outside the house, Keith looks at their car parked on the drive. Linda must have gone by her daughter's car.

Keith says, 'KLM 0TV. That's my car. K for Keith, L for Linda and M for Miller, my surname.'

And then adds quickly, 'T for Thomas, my father's name. And V for Violet, my mother's name.'

He then says, 'KLM is also the name of a plane, do you know? I used to fly in that a lot.'

'That's interesting. When did you last fly?' I ask again.

'Only a few months back,' he replies.

I know he won't be able to walk far. I help Keith get in my car.

In early October, the Indian summer is still lingering on a clear, sunny day. I decide to drive him to the Moor, as it will be impossible for a while to bring him there with the winter coming. The riot of colours on the trees is still there, although less spectacular than a couple of weeks back. Colourful leaves still tumbling to the ground with the wind. As we approach the creek, Keith asks me to stop. Outside, layers of soggy fallen leaves of various colours are on the road. I know it will be slippery, and just open the car window on his side.

'We cannot stop here for long. You can have a look outside the window.'

'All right then,' he says and sticks his head out of the window, smelling the soft foamy damp air outside.

Soon, we drive along and arrive at the car park on the Moor.

Keith struggles with his seat belt. I help to release it. Then slowly, he gets out of the car, holding on to my hand. We walk up carefully about twenty yards, Keith holding my hand with one and a walking stick on the other. Stunning view of the Moor and the valley below. I adjust his scarf and woolly hat. A new sparkle comes back in his eyes.

'Let's go up a bit,' he says.

'Only a little bit,' I know his knee is much worse now. He will suffer going down even a few steps, and it is windy here, although sunny.

Keith hums, walking up slowly, holding my hand with one and his walking stick on the other. He starts counting the cows in the field below as usual.

Then he sings again,

'Skin as white as precious pearl. She was my Tipperary girl.'

He tries but cannot remember the other lines and just repeats,

'Skin as white as precious pearl. She was my Tipperary girl,' again and again.

After a while, we drive back, Keith humming all the way.

I get an email from my volunteering group that Keith has passed away suddenly. Over the weekend, Linda had found him in bed writhing with pain. An ambulance was called, and he had emergency surgery at the hospital. He had died the same evening.

Silently, I shed tears for my friend. I go to the shop and get a condolence card. After writing the card, I stamp the envelope. I write Linda Miller on it.

Then I try to remember the address – it has entirely slipped from me for now.

Currently, more than 55 million people live with dementia worldwide, and nearly 10 million new cases are recorded yearly. One person every three minutes develop dementia in the UK - one in 14 people over 65 and 1 in 5 over 80 develop dementia.

So far, there is no cure.

These are people with locked-in memories who have contributed to our society, community, and their families. They leave behind many beautiful memories for us to treasure.

Cricket lover

Melbourne Airport 2015

'Maa, aapako chaay chaahie ya kofee? - Ma, do you want Chai or coffee?'

My ears pricked up with the Hindi conversation. I was nodding off at the departure lounge, waiting for our flights back to London from Melbourne. I looked up to find an old lady, about mid-seventy, slowly walking with her walking sticks to take a seat next to me.

'I will have coffee for a change, don't forget the milk and two sugars,' she shouted back towards her daughter and another woman, both in their forties. The old lady, most likely Indian in origin, slowly settled down in the seat next to me.

I noticed one of their luggage levels marked Kenya. In my broken Hindi, I asked her, 'have you been on holiday from Kenya to Australia?'

She replied in English, 'no, no, that's my daughter's sister-in-law's bag. She is from Kenya. I live in England. Well, we have been on a sort of holiday here. We have been following the Indian Cricket team in Australia and watching their world cup games.'

She elaborated that the three have been to all six games played by India in the qualifying round. They have travelled around Australia. They even went to New Zealand to see India's one match against them. They had watched India losing their semi-final in Sydney against Australia. Then they came to Melbourne as they had all the bookings and tickets for the world cup final. But as India was not playing, they did not go to watch the final and instead did some shopping before going home.

'You must be mad to go all the way to Melbourne from the UK and back, all within a week, just to watch the world cup final,' – I was told by many when I had announced my plan. I always had secretly felt a bit proud about my passion for cricket. I was not that good in the game, although I could bowl reasonably well. But over the last two decades, I started and captained the hospital cricket teams at the two hospitals where I worked. Now, I had sponsored two of my closest college friends to join me in this World Cup final – one from India and the other from the UK, who was returning with me. We had seen off the other friend for his flight to Kolkata only two hours back. But, sitting next to this elderly lady in Melbourne airport, I felt genuinely humbled.

As our flights were not due to leave for another couple of hours, we talked to her.

Her name was Rani. She was born in Nairobi, Kenya, in the 1940s. At that time, there were many Indian families in Nairobi, mainly from Gujarat and Punjab. Most of them were businessmen. Since 1920, when the British government finally officially declared Kenya as its colony, all of its subjects were considered British.

She remembered that when India became independent in 1947, her family and their friends often discussed moving back to India.

'Nairobi is no longer as it used to be. It is getting swamped with people moving in from the countryside every year. In the last ten years, the population of Nairobi has nearly doubled. Now there are slums everywhere,' said one of them.

'You can't blame them, though. Kenyans, mostly Kikuyu people, are often forced to work for meagre pay by the British farmers in the highlands. Everyone wants better opportunities for their family and their children, just like us,' Rani's father had replied.

But while they were planning to move back to India, the news of violent communal riots after the partition of India had put a stop to that. Families with young children had decided against going to such a volatile place. But then Kenya became more troublesome in the bid for its freedom from its British rulers, first with the militant Kenyan African Study Union and then with the Mau Mau rebel group.

With a few of their Gujrati and Punjabi friends, Rani's family decided to move to the nearby country of Uganda, where the cotton business was prospering more than in Kenya.

Uganda was also the most stable British colony in East Africa then. They already had business contacts there, and it did not take long to settle in Kampala and prosper with their own businesses. Rani and her elder brother were sent to the famous missionary Mengo Senior School. Her brother thrived at the school, but Rani did not enjoy the place.

'Too strict, everyone,' she smiled.

While her brother enrolled in the newly established National College of Business Studies in Makerere, Rani passed her final exam from her school with poor marks. She did not want to join the college. A local businessman's only son, Jiten, who was in his final year studying medicine at the Makerere Medical College, was found to be a match for Rani. They were soon married in a grand wedding ceremony.

'Both of you look Indian. Do you live in the UK now?' asked Rani.

'Yes, we were born in India but had been living in the UK for over thirty years,' I said.

'Which part of India were you from?'

'West Bengal. Villages near Kolkata.'

'What do you do in the UK?' she asked.

'We are both doctors,' my friend replied.

'As I mentioned, my husband was a doctor,' said Rani.

'Was?' I asked.

'He passed away from a heart attack two years back.,

We both said sorry to her and then sat silently for a while.

'Here is your Chai Ma,' her daughter came back. 'We could not find any snacks you would like. But we got some nuts,' she added and then looked at us.

Rani said to her, 'these are two Indian doctors from Kolkata.'

Her daughter said hello and then asked Rani if she would like to sit with us for a while or go to the duty-free shops with them. Rani replied that she would be happy to sit down and chat for now while resting her knees. Her daughter and her sister-in-law left for shopping.

Rani talked to us again between sipping her cup of tea.

'My husband, Jiten, absolutely loved cricket. He played for the medical college cricket team. But after he became a doctor, he did not get much time to play. Too busy!'

Soon after her husband Jiten had qualified as a doctor, the family had the chance to use their British passports for the first time when they went to London on holiday in 1969. One day, while his father talked to his business partners in the UK, Rani and her mother-in-law went around the Oxford Circus area for some shopping. Jiten went to the Lord's Cricket Ground to watch the England and West Indies test match. In the evening, he had talked excitedly about how lucky he was to see Gary Sobers, the best all-rounder in the world.

'But I really enjoyed the batting of young Clive Lloyd. He is going to be famous soon, I have no doubt,' he said.

The following day, after visiting the Natural History Museum, while walking by the Imperial College on the next street, Jiten had said, 'I hope one day I can come over here for my training.'

From London, they went to Leicester and met up with some of their Indian relatives who had settled in Leicester. They found that while many worked as train and bus drivers, some had started small businesses and were doing reasonably well. On their last evening in the UK, the four reflected on their luck with their lives back home in Uganda. They were already beginning to miss their large three-storey palatial house with five servants and two chauffeur-driven cars. All this was on top of their resorts in their plantations in the provincial towns. But Jiten's father reminded them that since the British colonial rule ended in 1961, under the leadership of Milton Obote, Uganda was moving into uncertain territory. Corruption was at its highest, and Obote ruthlessly turned against Asian businesses.

The family had taken a holiday in India in January 1971. They were impressed by how well some of their relatives were doing there and with the general confidence in India as an independent nation. Rani was most impressed by the opportunities Indian women had compared to what they faced in Eastern Africa. Jiten's father established many more business connections with the members of their extended families.

The week before they were due to leave India, the news arrived that Colonel Idi Amin had taken over from Milton Obote in a bloodless coup.

Initially, people believed Idi Amin's military government would stamp out bureaucracy and corruption. But looting and indiscriminate jailing of Asian traders increased. On 4 August 1972, Idi Amin announced his decision to rid the country of the 'bloodsucking' Asians he said were sabotaging the country's economy and taking away African jobs. His intention to rid the land of the 'British Asians' sent shockwaves around Uganda and the world. Amin gave the Asians ninety days to leave the country. He ordered the army to seize their property, homes, and businesses. After regular news of the military indecently assaulting them at checkpoints and not infrequently detaining them, women feared for their safety, leading to rape and murder.

Over dinner, Jiten and Rani's family talked about General Amin's decree. Rani's parents and her brother had more or less made up their minds about moving to India. Rani's in-laws were thinking the same, but Jiten said they would be better off going to the UK with their British passports.

'In the UK, I will have better prospects of finding decent training, hopefully in orthopaedics. And NHS is world-renowned,' said Jiten.

Soon Jiten's father agreed, 'true. We also know that, after all, the UK is a fair country. We are getting old now. But you, Rani, and hopefully your children in the future will have more opportunities there in your lives.'

'We all have British passports, and we have no choice but to leave this country anyway,' said Jiten.

'Idi Amin has already ordered the seizing of assets of all the Indian companies here,' agreed Rani's father.

Jiten and Rani's parents gave away most of their belongings, including their cars, except the gold ornaments and jewellery, to their Ugandan neighbours, friends, and their own long-serving servants. Rani's parents and her brother left for India five days later. Two days after them, Jiten's family hired a small truck to take mainly their personal belongings. They were one of the few lucky families to be able to book their flights soon after Amin's three-month expulsion notice. They hid all their jewellery inside Rani and her mother-in-law's clothes. Then they put on winter clothes on top of their shalwar kameez, pretending they needed all the warm clothes when arriving in England.

On the journey to the airport, there were several army checkpoints. Their luggage was searched, and some of the expensive clothes were looted. They were glad that Rani and her mother-in-law had hidden all the family jewellery under their clothes. But one of the commanders ripped the thin gold necklaces on their necks. Luckily, at the next army checkpoint, one of the officers recognised Jiten.

'I remember you, doctor. You looked after my mother only a few months back when she came to the hospital after fracturing her hip. I will come with you to the airport, doctor, to avoid any problem,' he declared and followed them to the airport's safety in his army truck.

Although they had booked tickets at the airport, they had to pay bribes to the official before finally boarding the plane for the UK. They eventually left Uganda, all of them with only the allowed fifty pounds in their possession.

On arrival at Stanstead Airport, they were met at the immigration checkpoint by officials from the resettlement board and scores of volunteers from many charities. The family was given temporary settlement at the newly opened Stradishall, an unused RAF air base. The families, who had already been shivering on the journey from the airport in late September, were grateful for the coats, sweaters, and knitted shawls distributed to them. Apparently, these were all donated by the local volunteers. After documentation and medical check-ups, they were taken to their allocated house, where the welcoming heating was already on.

Like many at the centre, although thankful for the generosity shown on their arrival, Jiten's family were keen to move out to start their new lives in the country as soon as possible. After discussion at the enquiry office, the family agreed to try to find somewhere to move in around Leicester, where some of their relatives lived.

Within a few weeks, the family moved to Leicester, where they were allocated a single-bedroom council house. Used to a luxurious lifestyle in Kampala, in the beginning, they found this place cramped but soon got used to it. Jiten found a job as a locum A&E doctor in the Leicester Hospital in the same month. Rani's father-in-law found that a childless elderly Gujarati couple, owners of a local Asian grocery shop and newsagent, was thinking of selling their business and retiring back in India.

Soon with a total of 100 pounds left in for the whole family after coming to the UK, they opened a joint account in the bank. They brought some of their jewellery to the bank a few days later. They were glad to find that the family's twenty-four-carat gold ornaments were worth enough to get the required loan to buy the business Jiten's father had in mind.

Jiten soon managed to get a six-month regular job in the A&E, while his father ran the grocery shop with the help of Rani and her mother-in-law. Luckily, most customers were Asians, and their scant English and thick accents did not matter.

In the first year of her arrival in the U.K, Rani became pregnant and later gave birth to her only daughter Meera. In the next few years, after trying unsuccessfully to get into higher training for orthopaedics, Jiten managed to become a full-time GP in the suburb of Leicester. Soon the family moved to a decent home just outside Leicester. Rani's father-in-law sold his shop, and the parents got busy visiting the local temple and making friends.

Jiten had joined the local cricket club and played on most Sundays. Rani, with her daughter, had sometimes gone to watch him play. Her mother-in-law died suddenly a few years later after a heart attack, and sadly, her father-in-law passed away within the year. Jiten soon became busier with his GP practice. With her daughter in school during the day, Rani became a telly addict. For some reason, she had found the test crickets on TV attractive. This also gave her something to discuss when Jiten returned home after his surgery. While she enjoyed test cricket, they both loved one-day cricket when it started in 1979. Often after dinner, they had sat together glued to the TV, watching the highlights from the one-day games.

In 1983, to everyone's surprise, India had easily beaten Australia to reach the world cup semi-final. Jiten, with his connections, had managed to get two tickets for the final match in Lord's when India played the West Indies.

'No one thought India had any chance against the mighty West Indies. But against all odds, India beat West Indies to become the world champion. And we were there,' proudly said, Rani.

'I watched the game on TV. After India scored only 183 runs, I thought the game was over. So I left for a walk with my dog, recording the rest of the game. I came back to find the most memorable day in world cricket. Kapil Dev's unbelievable catch to get Viv Richards out is still fresh in my memory,' I said.

'We have autographs of the 1983 Indian cricket team on a cricket bat in our house,' Rani said proudly.

'You are so lucky,' my friend replied.

Rani became hooked on watching any cricket match India has played since then. In 1993 they took a family holiday to India with their daughter Meera after her graduation with BA in economics. They had watched two full days of test cricket in Mumbai when India beat England by an innings and over a hundred runs. She soon became a Tendulkar fan, although Vinod Kambli scored over two hundred runs in that match.

Meera later joined a bank in London after doing a postgraduate degree in economics. Rani continued to say Meera, while working in the international section of her bank, had come across her future husband. A man from Uganda with Indian heritage. A year later, they got married. The woman with her now was her sister-in-law, who came to England for a family visit. Rani's son-in-law was hoping to come to Australia for the cricket world cup but had to cancel because of his last-minute work commitment.

Jiten and Rani had continued to follow cricket together whenever possible.

'We also watched Sourav Ganguly's India team winning the Nat West One Day series final at Lords in 2002. He famously took off his shirt and waved it from the balcony to celebrate – you will probably remember it because it caused so much controversy.'

'Yes. Everyone remembers that scene,' smiled my friend.

'We went to India in 2011 and watched in Mumbai, M.S.Dhoni as captain Indian team, win the Cricket World Cup for the second time,' Rani added.

'Unbelievable, you were in both the famous finals,' said my friend.

'You can write a book with a headline -Witness of the glorious moments of Indian cricket,' I said.

After sitting in silence for a while, Rani said that, unfortunately, Jiten died suddenly three months before they were due to watch the 2013 ICC Champions Trophy final in Edgbaston.

'We had the final tickets booked. I cried sitting next to the framed photograph of my husband in front of the TV watching M S Dhoni's India beat England.'

Three of us sat in silence for a while.

'Jiten had passionately discussed plans to come to Australia to watch the world cup final in Melbourne this year. He was confident that India would win. Then we would take a couple of months holiday in Australia,' Rani sighed.

After a while, she added, 'I decided to come here in his memory. I brought his photo with me. I carried it to all the venues so that I could watch the game together with him.'

She took out a framed photo from her handbag and showed it to us.

'But I know now it's not the same,' Rani said, holding back her tears.

Then in a hushed voice, she added, 'lately, I am forgetting certain things, mainly day-to-day things. I have told no one about it yet. That's the advantage of living alone myself, don't you think?

And luckily, every moment of my time with Jiten since our marriage is still there.' She pointed to her head.

We listened in silence while she added, 'in a way, it's easier to talk to a stranger about it. And you two seem to be decent people, plus doctors, and we will probably never meet again. I hear on the radio and TV a lot now about Alzheimer's. It worries me now that I am seventy-five years old, and after losing Jiten, I might end up forgetting him too.' She looked up at me.

I could only say, 'it may not be a bad idea to talk to your daughter about it and also contact an organisation like Alzheimer's Society for advice.'

Her daughter with her sister-in-law had come back by then and pointed at the large screen. Our flights were at gate 15.

*'What is human life but a game of cricket?'
said Brian Lara, the famous West Indian batsman
in 2005. It remains true for billions in their lives.*

*Cricket is the second most popular sport in the
world, after football. Worldwide around 2.5
billion people follow it regularly. Many of these
fans are of Asian origin from countries such as
India, Pakistan, Sri Lanka and Bangladesh.*

Money over health

Khichan, Rajasthan March 2017

Bird watching season in Khichan was nearly over. This has been an excellent season for the locals. Over the last four months, busloads of bird watchers from all over India had travelled fifty kilometres from the fort city of Jodhpur in Rajasthan. Many had stayed a few nights at the 15th century Phalodi Town, known as the Salt City, in the buffer zone of the Thar Desert, only five kilometres from the Khichan village. Several decades ago, many wealthy traders lived in Khichan. But today, all of them have migrated to metropolitan cities like Delhi, Madras, Mumbai or Kolkata. 18th-century Lal Niwas, a palace made of red sandstone, was now a popular hotel. The town itself was a popular tourist attraction with many temples, including the attractive 19th Century

Parashnath Glass Temple and the Sun Temple next to the ruins of the three-hundred-year-old Phalodi Fort. Like in Khichan village, most of the Havelis - mansion houses, lay empty in this town.

From all around the world, bird watchers, however, came here only to go to Khichan, now known as the Demoiselle Crane Village. These migratory cranes are so-called because of their delicate and maiden-like appearance. They arrive in Khichan between September and March. The cranes flock to this sleepy village tucked away in the corner of the Thar Desert in large numbers in the winter months, making an amazing spectacle. Just after the monsoon rains have ceased, these unique bird species fly in from their breeding grounds on the plains and steppes of Eurasia and Mongolia. In the evenings, the sky darkens as the cranes fly back to their resting grounds in the village. The air reverberates with their trumpeting call and the rush of air through curved wings as they glide to land.

Local volunteers have been feeding these birds around the village pond, one of the few water sources in this arid land, for over fifty years. Now the number of birds touches a staggering fifteen thousand each year. Besides these dainty cranes, grey heron, great egret, northern pintail, northern shoveler, black-winged stilts, Temminck's stint, tufted duck, spotted redshank, common redshank, common sandpiper, rock pigeons, white-throated kingfisher, Indian pond heron, and other species of birds can be sighted at Khichan making the place a birdwatcher's dreamland.

Harshal had two souvenir shops, one in his homeplace Khichan and the other in Phalodi town. While he managed the busier shop in Phalodi by himself, his wife, with her younger brother ran the shop in the village. In a way, Harshal was glad that the tourist season was ending in Khichan. His wife, Anju, was just over eight months pregnant with their first baby. Secretly they had already thought about the name for the baby, although it was not the tradition. Tarak, if it was a boy and Aasha, if it was a girl. Both of Harshal's brothers had only boys. He wished the new baby was a girl.

Now that they had made some money, Harshal had arranged for Anju to have a check-up with a proper doctor in Phalodi. Some have mentioned a new nursing home with an expert gynaecologist who had moved from Jodhpur only a year back. Only the day before, the nurses at the village health centre said that at 34 weeks of her pregnancy, Anju was doing very well, and everything was going well. Still, Harshal wanted to have a proper check-up with a specialist.

In the newly built nursing home, more building works were going on the one side. After paying upfront the consultation fee, more than a week of their families' earnings, they waited in the small half-empty waiting room for nearly twenty minutes. Soon they were called in by a nurse.

A middle-aged doctor then examined Anju with a constantly concerned face. While Anju was still on the examining table, the doctor sat opposite Harshal, writing some notes for a few minutes. Then, after finishing his writing and moving the notes away, he looked at Harshal with a concerned look.

'I am very worried for the baby,' he said.

Harshal's world almost stopped, but he somehow managed to ask, 'why? What's wrong with the baby?'

Anju tried to sit up from the examining couch hearing this, but the nurse restrained her. The doctor replied in a calm voice that she must have a caesarean section operation immediately for the baby's sake.

'But the nurses at the health centre only yesterday said everything was going well,' Harshal tried to protest.

'They are not specialists,' the gynaecologist replied.

'But I have no pain,' Anju shouted from the bed.

The nurse shushed her while the doctor explained to Harshal that without an immediate operation, there is a serious risk to both the baby and the mother.

Harshal asked the doctor, 'then what can you do? How much would it cost?'

The doctor, without any hesitation, said, 'it's going to be twenty-five thousand rupees plus any cost of additional medicines.'

Shell shocked, Harshal said, 'we don't have that kind of money. Shall I take her to the government hospital in town?'

'It is up to you. But time is crucial here. And you know how dirty the hospital is, and there is probably no gynaecologist on duty this evening.'

Then, immediately the doctor added, 'you know there is a government health insurance scheme which came in only the last few years. As a low earner, you can get up to 30,000 rupees from the state for one year's emergency medical expenses.'

'But that will take ages with the paperwork in the town office, which is closed now anyway,' replied Harshal.

'No. You only need to sign some forms with me here now. Then I can do the operation immediately,' said the gynaecologist.

Within the next half an hour, Anju was rushed to the operation room while Harshal waited alone in the waiting room. Then, another forty-five minutes later, another doctor wearing a green gown and a blue hat came outside to talk to him.

'I am the anaesthetist,' he said.

Harshal jumped up from his seat. 'How is Anju? How is the baby?' he asked.

'The mother is alright. She is still under anaesthesia. We are extremely concerned about the baby; her APGAR score is only 5.'

'What does that mean?' Harshal's heart was thumping by now. He could hardly breathe.

'She needs help with her breathing. We don't have the facility here. You have to take her to a hospital with baby unit immediately,' said the anaesthetist.

A nurse then brought the newborn wrapped up in a blanket and handed it over to Harshal. Completely stunned, Harshal ran downstairs, cradling the baby in his arms. Luckily a taxi was just dropping off some visitors at the nursing home. Within ten minutes, they reached the Government hospital. Harshal ran to the emergency department holding the baby, only to be told there was no doctor there this evening. The nurses there advised him that in the charity hospital near Khichan village, an outsider team of anaesthetists and surgeons were working for the week. They might be able to help.

Harshal made the 5 km trip to the charity hospital in the same taxi, looking at his daughter's beautiful pale blue face all the way. He rushed through the door at the charity hospital, holding a newborn in his arms. Luckily, the volunteering team of surgeons and two anaesthetists were waiting by the reception area at the end of their day's work before going for dinner.

The baby looked blue, and the two anaesthetists took the baby immediately to the emergency room with oxygen.

Shattered looking, Harshal said, 'my wife, the mother, does not yet know anything about all this. She is still under anaesthesia in the nursing home and has not even seen our first child.'

After a few minutes, one of the anaesthetists came out and said the baby needed to be ventilated immediately. Unfortunately, the charity hospital in Khichan was not equipped to deal with neonates. The only option was to take the baby to the nearest neonatal unit in Jodhpur, 50km away. The hospital arranged an ambulance immediately with an oxygen mask for the baby.

As the baby with her father was taken away, it was clear that the baby was unlikely to survive the journey.

The colleagues at the charity hospital said that these tragic situations were now happening frequently. To ease the burden on the rural poor, the Indian government launched a National Health Insurance scheme in 2008. Under the project, families living below the poverty line can receive treatment worth up to 30,000 rupees ($550) each year from designated private hospitals, which the hospitals can claim directly from the state. With this new scheme, unscrupulous doctors were doing many unnecessary operations only to make money. There are now mad rushes by them to earn as much money as possible to do these unwarranted surgeries, frightening the relatives as if they were genuine emergencies.

One of them said, 'recent reports showed that these unscrupulous private doctors had pushed hundreds of young women in their twenties to have unnecessary hysterectomies for only heavy bleeding during menstruation! It made headline news, but sadly not much has changed yet.'

Tears ran down our cheeks, still thinking of the newborn and her parents.

In recent decades countries such as India have seen a sharp rise in private health care, often beyond the reach of ordinary people. In 2020, private infrastructure accounted for nearly 62% of India's health infrastructure. Currently, private infrastructure accounts for nearly 62% of India's health infrastructure. Currently, India has 43,486 private hospitals (1.18 million beds), while there are only 25,778 public hospitals (just over 713,000 beds).

The number of unnecessary surgical operations worldwide varies from 30% to above when many surgeries are performed simply for profit making.

Ayushman Bharat, a National Health Protection Scheme launched by the Government of India in 2008, aimed to support low-income families with coverage up to Rs. 5 Lakh per family annually for hospital treatment. A BBC interview in 2013 recorded that thousands of Indian women were having their wombs removed unnecessarily, only performed to make money for unscrupulous private doctors.

American Medical Association, as early as 1976, called for a congressional hearing on the same subject. They claimed, '2.4 million unnecessary operations performed (annually) on Americans at the cost of $3.9 billion, and 11,900 patients had died from the unnecessary operations.' But even in the last decade, over 11% of all surgeries are considered unnecessary in the country.

Money over health

Yacuiba, Bolivia August 2016

The eight-hour car journey from Tarija through the mountain road to Yacuiba was often scary but breathtaking. Massive cactuses on the sloping hills added to the beautiful view of the undulating hills beyond. At only 3km from the Argentine border, Yacuiba, with over 90,000 population, was a major commercial centre, close to the profitable gas and oil industry. With wide streets lined by many colonial buildings and large, beautiful parks, Yacuiba looked prosperous from the outside.

On arrival at the only government hospital, an army band played welcome songs, surprising our visiting volunteering team. A big welcome meeting with the hospital staff, town mayor, local officials, and the local MP, followed by hat and poncho gifts. After a tour of the hospital, I realised this place had 10 surgeons with appropriate anaesthetic support covering different specialities. More than in my last hospital in the NHS in the UK! I wondered, what was I doing here?

Soon talking to the local health officials, it became clear. The surgeons were making excuses for not having enough keyhole surgery equipment in the government hospital to do gallbladder surgery. They were hinting to patients to go to their private hospitals in the town for these operations. The average daily income for the country was just over 20 US Dollars. But around here, like in the rest of the country, one in three lived below the poverty level, and one in six lived in extreme poverty, unlike a few wealthy people benefiting from the commercial boom in hydrocarbon exploitation nearby. There was no way most could afford the costs in the private hospitals.

Gallstone diseases were common in females in Bolivia, especially those with a history of multiple pregnancies, as were around the world. In a mainly Catholic country like Bolivia, contraception was not a choice. As a result, many young women, some in their late teens, became pregnant here, and gallstone was prevalent. Most suffered pain, but some also suffered complications needing hospital admissions, often more than once. A small number of these patients end up with life-threatening complications.

Unfortunately, many patients in the Yacuiba area had waited up to over four years to have any gall bladder surgery and had suffered many complications. Ordinary people in the town and the surrounding areas did not have enough money to pay for private nursing home fees for the necessary operation, even though their livelihoods were frequently cut short by the illness.

Local officials had not wanted to upset the surgeons in their only hospital in the area. After an entire afternoon meeting with the ministry, hospital director, local surgical team and myself, I was proud of my negotiating skill. They allowed us to go ahead with working in the hospital.

The local health authority already had a list of waiting patients. Some had come from a far distance, as the local radio had announced my arrival well beforehand. After seeing the patients in the evening, we scheduled them for age-old and tested standard open gall bladder surgery. The main difference between the keyhole surgery and the standard open operation for gallstone disease is 2-3 days more stay in the hospital and a couple of extra weeks recovering at home.

Our routine became an early morning start for the next few days, operating all day. Then an evening clinic to see some more patients and back to the hotel around 9 pm. Several of the patients were in their early twenties and had left their babies at their homes with their own parents. There were also some late teenage patients, one with a two-year-old baby at home.

Late one evening was a mouth-watering Argentine-style barbecue in the local MP's house with all the dignitaries. After many thank you speeches, they asked me to speak and give my recommendations as an outsider expert about why the local hospital did not work so well for the poor.

Without holding back, I said the authorities needed to enforce a better work ethic on the local team, who seemed to be only interested in making money in their private clinics. Everyone raised their glasses to it.

On my last day, I finished operating just after noon. We had to leave for the return eight-hour journey to Tarija. The hospital surprised me with a big farewell and thank you party in the long corridor. A few of my patients, including some I had operated on only the day before, had heard of this. To everyone's surprise, they had walked the corridors only to come for this. Some of them were still holding their tummy with one hand over their stitches while they came. They wanted to be there to thank me publicly.

When they hugged me, tears flooded our eyes.

In 2010, under President Evo Morales, the country's first indigenous president, Bolivia created a free Unified Health System providing health coverage to 70% of the population. Within a decade, Under-5 mortality was halved.

But inequalities in healthcare continue for other reasons. For example, the large Government Hospital in Yacuiba of 97,296 people has 10 full-time surgeons (including different specialities). But the town also has 5 private hospitals where these surgeons work / part-own and often coax patients to have their treatment there. A familiar story of private healthcare around the world.

Death of a humanitarian
Masanga. Sierra Leone 2019

The gold mine in Masanga stood on the opposite side of the Pampana river from Masanga Hospital. Gold mining has been a relatively small industry in Sierra Leone compared with diamonds and iron ore. Like many African countries, Sierra Leone had courted foreign companies, which paid governments small fees for mining rights and made most of the profits. But locals benefited very little. The mine workers got paid only a bit more than those working in the agricultural fields.

Approximately half a million people depend on Masanga Hospital for their healthcare. Masanga Hospital started as a Leprosy Hospital in the 1960s. During the terrible 'civil war' between 1991 and 2002, the rebels used the hospital as a base. It was eventually forced to close in 1997. In the face of all this, the village people of Masanga kept their hope and continued to maintain the hospital grounds.

After the war, in 2006, with a partnership between several European charitable organisations and agreement from the Government of Sierra Leone, the hospital was rebuilt to provide emergency surgical, obstetric, and paediatric care and general healthcare for over twelve thousand patients every year. Free healthcare is offered to under-fives, pregnant women, and locals of limited means. It also provided emergency surgical training to 16 community health officers (CHO) annually and trained over 300 nurses yearly.

The hospital's only doctor was from the international Capacare Organisation. Wouter Willem Eric Nolet from Holland, who had previously volunteered in Surinam, had travelled from Holland to Freetown, nearly 8500 km, in an old SAB with a friend. In the car's boot, he brought a state-of-the-art 3-D printer. Previously during volunteering in Suriname, Wouter had seen no prosthesis available for the many amputees following the 'civil war' in that country. He wanted to manufacture prostheses through his 3D printer for the poor community in Sierra Leone. After spending a few months in a charity hospital around Free Town, he has moved to Masanga as the hospital's programme coordinator and only doctor.

Within a year, Wouter excelled. He led and developed the local organisation, planned student rotations, organised courses, trained surgical CHOs, hosted international trainers, and communicated with the health ministry and other stakeholders. These were on top of working as the only trained doctor in Masanga Hospital.

I had a chance to meet Wouter in Masanga in April 2019. Between my visits to Sierra Leone, I had contacted the Norwegian charity CapaCare. They were running the programme of emergency surgical training for the CHOs, similar to the programme in Ethiopia we had initiated. After a few earlier phone calls with Wouter, he was delighted with my offer to give these essential healthcare specialists additional skills training. He invited me to run a two-day skills course in Masanga.

Volunteers stayed in the 'UK House,' only a five-minute walk from the hospital by the river opposite the gold mine. The tin hut accommodation was rudimentary, and there was no electricity for the duration of my stay. But to our relief, in this oppressive heat, at least we had buckets of cold water to wash. A lady came from the village to cook food for us on an open fire. After a brief tour of the facilities, in the evening with candlelight, I had a long chat with the Wouter, a 32year old medic. He had been in Masanga by then for the last few years. He was the only medically qualified surgeon for the hospital.

Wouter's passion for improving the country's surgical care impressed me. He spoke fervently about the discrepancy of healthcare in resource-poor countries compared to the unnecessary wastage in the developed world. He also spoke about his frustration in dealing with the inefficiency and bureaucracy at the Sierra Leone Government level.

I have travelled worldwide and worked in many developing countries' health care. In those couple of hours, we talked until the candlelight ran out. I was touched by this young man's zeal for making a difference in the lives of ordinary people. It was raining, and soon we retired to bed. Wouter reminded me to tuck my mosquito nets properly.

Apart from the mosquitos, there were occasional stray rats, and Lhasa fever had not gone away! At night, I woke up with intermittent loud banging noises on the tin roof. The next morning, I realised they were from mangoes falling on the roof from overhanging trees! Then, as I collected some, a few local children came also to gather, and we had some laughs.

Later at the hospital, I was amazed by how easily Wouter was accepted by everyone, from patients, nurses, cleaners, and surgical trainees alike, as if he was one of their own. Soon Wouter said goodbye to me as he had to drive to Freetown to negotiate with the ministry about some overdue support for Masanga Hospital. The staff said to me, 'he is our own very special Sierra Leonean.'

I never met him again.

In early November of the same year, after returning from my visit to another part of Sierra Leone, I had a shocking email from Capacare Charity. I learnt that on 11th November night, a lady with obstructed delivery had come to Masanga Hospital from a long distance. By the time she arrived, she was bleeding from all her orifices. Trying to save the baby and the mother, Wouter had done an emergency caesarean section within the hour. Unfortunately, the mother died soon after, although the baby had survived.

The next day Wouter had to go to another town where he was running a training course. In the evening, he had a high fever. Initially, he had thought he had contracted malaria again. But the fever had persisted, and he had worsened. He was taken to a hospital in Freetown, but his condition continued to deteriorate.

In the next few days, they transferred him by air ambulance to his home country Holland. After eleven days in the ICU in his country of birth, Wouter sadly passed away from Lhasa fever. His assistant for the caesarean section, a final year female medical student from another country on elective placement, had also contracted Lhasa fever but, after two weeks in the ICU in her country, fortunately, had recovered.

Wouter was only 32 years of age.

Sierra Leone, with 8 million people, has one of the lowest life expectancies in the world - only 55yrs. Although improving, still 14 mothers are dying in every hundred childbirths, and about 13 children out of every hundred born do not reach their fifth birthday. It is one of the poorest countries in the world despite its rich reserves of gold, diamond and other minerals being exploited by rich countries.

Lassa fever remains endemic in parts of Sierra Leone, with confirmed 15 cases in 2019, 22 in 2018 and 30 in 2017.

The twins

Bermejo, Bolivia. 2016

Phillipa, our local coordinator, invited me to join their team on a Sunday to go to Bermejo, where they ran a mobile health clinic and an orphanage. From the provincial city of Tarija, we drove between beautiful mountain gorges to the small town for over three hours. A shallow river full of fish separated Bermejo from Argentina. The half of a bridge over the river was marked with a Bolivian horizontal tricolour of red, yellow, and green. The other half was with Argentina's light blue at the top and bottom with white in the middle. While a few trucks crossed the bridge, many people carried their merchandise back and forth on the river.

The mobile clinic site was in an agricultural field amongst Bermejo's extensive sugarcane fields and factories. Thousands of migrant workers from as far as La Paz came here for seasonal work. The clinic promoted disease prevention while providing vaccination, medical and dental care and psychological counselling. After spending most of the day there, we visited the nearby orphanage sponsored by the charity on our way back.

The orphanage looked after thirty children between six months to sixteen years old. The carer teacher asked the older children to say a few words in English to me. They did it beautifully. The children then asked me to sing a nursery rhyme in English. I sang 'Twinkle, twinkle little star' as best I could, and they loved it. Twin girls in the orphanage, about five years old, almost the same age as my twin granddaughters, caught my attention.

Their mother came there for her regular once-weekly visit to help clean and cook at the orphanage while spending a day with her children. When she learnt that I, too, have twin grandchildren, she wanted to talk to me. Then, through my translator, I heard her story.

Twenty-five-year-old Grecia was also born as a twin. Her sister Mariana was older by one hour. The traditional custom was for the father to take the weaker looking one outside and kill. This allowed the mother to return to work in the field with one newborn tied to her back only a couple of days after childbirth, sometimes the next day. It was not practical to have twins. But their father had gone against this. My translator, at this point, explained that infanticide has been outlawed in Bolivia for the last few years.

Despite the difficulties, Grecia's parents managed to bring up the girls to the age of four. But then their father died in an accident in the sugar cane factory. Struggling to cope, their mother had brought them to this same orphanage. Mariana had blossomed at the local school. But from her pre-teenage years, Grecia had hated the daily routine of the orphanage and the convent school. She had ended up in many troubles with other children and even with her teachers at school. After her blunt refusal to go to the Sunday mass for several weeks, reluctantly, their mother had taken Grecia out of the orphanage at the age of thirteen. While Mariana remained in the orphanage, Grecia went to work in the field with her mother.

Soon, while age fourteen, Grecia joined her mother and others going across the slow-flowing Bermejo Rive to the Argentinian border town of Aguas Blancas to ferry goods. The river, at its narrowest, is only 100 m wide and shallow in most places.

In the beginning, walking over the river to cross to a different town was like an adventure for Grecia. Less populated than Bermejo, Aguas Blancas was the best place to find colourful fabrics, second-hand clothing, and other merchandise brought from the Chilean ports. While the road bridge only one kilometre away had customs and immigration controls for the buses and cars travelling through it, crossing the river on foot avoided all of that. Undoubtedly, the customs knew all about it but kept a blind eye as it profited both sides.

Grecia had been doing this twice a month with her mother for a few years. In the meantime, Mariana had been doing well at the orphanage and school. She was then sent to a boarding school attached to a convent for free in Tarija. There she had done exceptionally well before going to college.

On one of their trips over the river in the strong current after heavy rain the night before, their mother had slipped one day. Grecia was by her mother's side. Luckily, with the help of the others, their mother was pulled out of the river. She could not stand up and was taken to the local hospital on a stretcher. The local doctors had said their mother had broken her hip bone and needed a major operation. They transferred her the next day to Tarija. Three days after the surgery, while Mariana had a chance to visit her for the first time at the hospital, unfortunately, their mother had suddenly collapsed and died. Her body was brought to their village in Bermejo for burial. Mariana could not come because she hardly had any money.

At sixteen, Grecia had become the only earner, managing her affairs and also sending small amounts of money to her older sister, still in college. Soon Grecia started again going across the river every week. She always tried to get to Aguas Blancas early to get to the best price traders to open. She would then rush back to sell them to another trader in Bermejo. She was making just about enough money to buy food to make a thick broth of Jak'a lawa of ground corn cooked with potatoes and fish. It was only a miserable gain from her sales for a whole day's work, but it was less hard labour than working in the fields with a little more money. And working on the farms was only seasonal.

Mariana, with no money, had managed to come to Bermejo only twice in the few years when one of the nuns from the convent was visiting this area.

In the middle of June, just before her eighteenth birthday, Grecia was making an early morning trip to Aguas Blancas. The sky was heavy with clouds from the morning. While she was on the other side, it had rained heavily. On the way back to Bermejo, Grecia almost slipped on the stream. Ernesto, a year older and wading nearby, had grabbed her in time before she lost her merchandise. Her mother's fall in the river immediately came to Grecia's mind. After getting back on the shore in Bermejo, Grecia, all wet head to toe, had been treated to a very welcome coffee from a local vendor by Ernesto.

Over the months, their romance had blossomed. Ernesto had often spent nights at Grecia's. In a strictly Catholic country, there was no question of any contraception. After living in sin for almost a year, Grecia found herself pregnant. Although against the religion, in the first few weeks, she had tried herbal drugs suggested by some and fortunately had an abortion. But after only ten months, despite being extra careful, she became pregnant again. This time, however, herbal drugs did not end her pregnancy and continued.

Ernesto, as a decent man, had married Grecia in a brief church ceremony when she was seven months pregnant. Grecia gave birth later to twin girls, Yana and Inti. She was overjoyed with emotion to see their beautiful faces and relieved at the same time that she had not died at childbirth like one of her neighbours only a month back.

Ernesto was astounded rather than happy with the twins. Initially, he had tried to be supportive but gradually became distant. There were rumours around that he was seeing other women in Bermejo. Soon Grecia was being beaten up by her husband for trivial reasons. As if Ernesto was trying to smother his anger with a storm of blows on Grecia. But no matter how hard he hit her, it could never draw any tear from Grecia. She would howl like a cornered animal and roll on the ground with no tears.

Before their twin's first birthday, Ernesto had moved away to Tarija to live with another woman while working as a street vendor.

Grecia had struggled hard to earn any living while looking after her twins. Mariana, by now, had joined a college and worked as a part-time teacher in the convent. From time to time, she had sent some money to Grecia, but it was never enough. Unable to cope, when the twins were three years old, Grecia brought them to this orphanage. It had broken her heart, and in the beginning, she often questioned whether she had done the right thing for her children. But then, during her visits, she had found the children were happy and well-nourished, which had made her less guilty.

Within a year, she had started working for free one day a week at the orphanage. She feels that this gives her more contact with her girls growing up. Grecia added Mariana is now a full-time teacher in Tarija and works for free at an orphanage in the City on Sundays.

It was time for us to leave for Tarija. Grecia went to fetch Yana and Inti to say a proper goodbye before we left.

In Bolivia, of nine million people, a quarter lives in extreme poverty. This, combined with no contraception and abortion being illegal because of mainly catholic religion, many children are abandoned soon after birth. Currently, almost as much as 10% of all children in Bolivia are orphans. Most of the orphanages are supported by international charities.

Handkerchief

Sucre, Bolivia. 2016

The night bus from Tarija in southern Bolivia had travelled nearly 500 km north to Sucre while I slept.

Built during the colonial era, in the early morning sunshine, Sucre looked grand with beautiful vast plazas, streets organised in a grid, Andalusian architecture houses and churches in white. Sucre remains the constitutional capital of Bolivia, while La Paz is the de facto capital. After dropping off our luggage at the hotel and a quick breakfast, a car sent by the hospital drove us there.

The drive from the city centre to the hospital took almost an hour. The hospital was one of the three in the city serving a 300,000 population. In the hospital, at the medical director's office, was the usual welcome and introduction meeting. They appreciated some of the essential items I managed to bring with me as a donation.

As I was due to leave the office, the shy-looking secretary approached my local translator and whispered something.

My translator said, 'she was asking if she could come to see you in your clinic later. She heard that you are also a breast surgeon. She has some breast problem.'

'Sure. But I would be operating all day today and tomorrow. The best time may be tomorrow lunchtime between operating,' I replied.

The next day at lunchtime, I found an empty room in the outpatient clinic. With my translator lady and a nurse, I talked to the secretary woman. Her name was Kantuta.

'What a lovely name. Does it mean anything?' I asked.

She spoke to my translator with a smile on her face.

'Kantuta is a sacred flower for the Aymara, and the national flower of Bolivia, also known as the 'flower of the Incas.' This name denotes beauty and purity. She is from the Aymara tribe,' my translator interpreted.

It turned out this 28-year-old lady had found a lump in her breast over a year back. Working in the hospital, she was more conscious of it. In the last few weeks, she has been seen by the local surgeons who had carried out tests, including a needle biopsy, privately. She was warned it was likely cancer and advised an urgent operation in their private hospital. She did not have enough money at present. She wanted to know from me if she could wait a few months while she managed to find the money or if I could do the operation for her while I was in Sucre.

With my chaperone, I examined her. Then I checked all her reports, including her biopsy. There was no suggestion of any cancer. It was a benign condition and not even precancerous. I reassured her, and she started sobbing with relief. Usually, when I am in a clinic, I have a tissue box on my table for such a situation. But there was none here. I gave her my handkerchief to wipe her tears. She hugged me and left.

In the next few days, whenever I had to come to the medical director's office, the young secretary always welcomed me with the broadest smile.

On my last working day in the hospital, I was leaving at about five pm to go to the building opposite to teach the residents for another hour. Kantuta came up to me. She said, 'I will see you tomorrow before you leave.'

I said, 'no, it was my last day. I will leave Sucre early in the morning.'

She said nothing and left.

After teaching the residents, I was back at my hotel in the city centre around 9 pm. An hour later, after having our dinner, I was packing my rucksack in my room for my journey early the following day. The telephone rang in my room. It was the hotel reception - someone to see me at the desk. Surprised, but I came down there soon.

Waiting there was Kantuta with her lovely smile. She returned my handkerchief, washed and ironed. Then she handed me her gift of three embroidered handkerchiefs she had made for me. The embroidery in Spanish read, 'Gracias. Con amor desde Sucre - Thank you. With love from Sucre.'

She had taken at least two changes of buses at this time of the night to come to my hotel, just to say thank you!

She gave me another hug, and now I needed a handkerchief.

Sucre was founded in 1538 by a Spanish conquistador. Its narrow streets of the city centre, organised in a grid, reflect the Andalusian culture. On May 25, 1809, the Bolivian independence movement against the colonists started here with the ringing of the bell of the Basilica of Saint Francisco. This bell was rung to the point of breakage, but it can still be seen in the Basilica.

Only 5 km outside Sucre are the most extensive collection in the world of more than 5,000 visible dinosaurs footprints, including the world's longest recorded baby T-Rex tracks, measuring 350m.

Anniversary

Julian parked his car in the Countryman Pub car park and looked at his watch. Five minutes before seven. He hated being late. Before going inside, he looked for Elizabeth's car, but it was not there. Their friend Barry and Bev's white land rover was already there. Julian rushed inside. After using the toilet to wash his hands, he met their friend by the bar.

'Sorry, it was touch and go at the surgery. We had a meeting after work, and I thought it would go on forever. Do you both want another drink?' Julian asked as he ordered his pint of lager.

'No thanks. Our glasses are still almost full,' replied Beverly.

'Shall we go inside? Liz should be here soon. As you both know, she is Mrs Punctuality! She should have been back home from Yoga class by six.'

With their drinks, three of them went to the half-empty restaurant section. A young waiter, probably still in his college, showed them to a table by the window reserved for the four.

'NHS is crumbling, and we all get the feeling that the Government wants it that way,' said Julian as he sipped his lager. 'Anyway, enough talk about my work. How are you two? Any news from Rosalyn? You must be super excited about having your first grandchild.'

'She is due next week. But you know these things can happen earlier or a few days later,' replied Beverly.

Julian looked at his watch. It was ten past seven. He apologised to their friends for Beverly not being there yet and sent a text to her. After another few minutes, he sent another text. No reply. Then after waiting for another minute, he said to his friends, 'I don't know why Liz is late. She is not replying to my texts. Maybe a problem with her mobile. Very sorry. I am going to call her on the landline by the bar.'

Calls to their landline and Elizabeth's mobile went answered. Julian returned to his friend and said he was worried about Elizabeth and would drive home to check.

'Please order your food. We will be here in 15-20 minutes max and catch up with you,' he said before leaving.

Back at home, Elizabeth's car was in her usual parking place. Julian rushed inside to find Elizabeth sprawled on the sofa, watching TV in her pyjamas.

'We were supposed to have dinner with Bev and Barry at seven in Countryman this evening. Why are you still home?'

'Dinner with Bev and Barry? Tonight?'

'Yes. You arranged with Bev a few days back. And you reminded me this morning before I left for work. Never mind. Get dressed quickly. They are still waiting there.' Julian then texted Barry that they were on their way.

Their wedding anniversary this year was on the first Saturday in April. Their son Michael arrived early on Friday with his wife Emma and their two children, ten-year-old Bernie and three-year-old Tim. Bernie came out of the car as soon it had stopped. After giving big hugs to Elizabeth and Julian, she gave them a card she had made for their wedding anniversary. Tim was fast asleep in the car. Julian gently picked him up and took him straight to their bedroom.

Late the next morning, their eldest daughter Bella arrived with her husband, Richard. They would be spending a few days with Julian and Elizabeth as they were due to move to Australia next month.

While they were all having tea in their garden, the telephone inside the house rang. Julian went to answer. It was their second daughter Millie. She could not come this weekend for the family gathering as she was working. She was ringing to wish them a happy anniversary.

'Happy anniversary Dad. Sorry I could not come this year. I tried both your mobiles with no answers.'

'Thanks, Luv. Sorry, we left both our mobiles in the kitchen. We are outside and enjoying the sun. I will get your Mum now. See you soon. Take care. Love you.'

Barry brought the cordless phone outside and handed it over to Elizabeth.

Elizabeth held the phone to her ear and said, 'Hello.' Then said, 'thank you,' before switching off the phone. She said to others at the table, 'I don't know who that was. Sounded young. Any way more tea or coffee, anybody?'

'That was Millie! You cut her off. She wanted to speak to others,' said Julian.

'Who is Millie?' asked Elizabeth.

'Are you joking?' said Julian.

The mobile Julian had carried back to the garden a minute ago rang.

'Mum cut me off. What's wrong with her? Is she angry that I could not come this weekend?'

Julian handed over the phone to Elizabeth. 'It's Millie,' he said.

'Hello, darling. How are You? How is work? Are you coming next weekend?' asked Elizabeth. Then she chatted on the phone for several minutes.

'Does anyone want more tea or coffee?' Elizabeth asked while gathering the empty cups and the teapot.

'I will give you a hand, Liz,' said Emma and got up.

'Tim and Bernie. Do you want hot chocolate?' shouted Elizabeth. The two of them came running towards her from the swing.

Bella waited until the four of them had gone inside and said, 'she did that to me a couple of weeks back. I had to phone her on landline because she was not answering her mobile. She did not know who I was.' Then looking towards the kitchen, she quietly asked, 'is she alright, Dad?'

Julian did not want to worry his children and did not say that it had also happened to him a few times in the last few months.

Since retiring as deputy headmaster of the local comprehensive school the year before, Elizabeth had developed a busy social life. Apart from Yoga class, swimming, and walking group, she joined a book club a few months back. She has started painting again after almost forty years. Elizabeth was now also a keen gardener as well. Until her retirement, Elizabeth shared cooking 60/40 with Julian. But now, she insisted that she would do most of the cooking except on rare occasions. Julian did not mind as she was always the better cook, and now with time in her hand, she produced new delicacy most week.

As a semi-retired GP, seventy-two-year-old Julian was now working only three sessions a week with no night or weekend on-calls. He has joined the local badminton club, playing in the evening once weekly. Surprisingly, even after all these years, he had easily fitted in well with the club's younger members. With time in their hands, Elizabeth and Julian now travelled more, in the country and abroad.

After playing badminton, one evening, Julian returned home after seven. The TV was on in the living room, but no sign of Elizabeth. He went to the kitchen. One of the hobs on the gas cooker was burning full-on with nothing cooking.

'Liz,' he shouted. 'You have left the gas on. Where are you?'

After having no answer, he quickly looked through the window towards their back garden. No one was there. He switched off the gas and went upstairs. The TV was on in their bedroom, and Elizabeth was in bed under a blanket, half asleep.

Julian went downstairs and defrosted some food for their dinner while thinking about how soon he could arrange for Elizabeth to be seen by one of his colleagues. He had no doubt that she was showing early signs of dementia and thought he needed to arrange a GP appointment.

But the next few days were already planned. They travelled to Ealing near London, where their daughter Bella and her husband lived. Julian and Elizabeth would spend a couple of days together with Bella and Richard before their permanent move to Australia. Four of them enjoyed the time, and Julian and Elizabeth reminisced the time of Bella's growing up. One evening they all went to a Westend theatre in London.

Elizabeth reminisced about the first time she and Julian came to the theatre next door almost forty years back to see Les Miserable. Then she gave Julian a gentle kiss.

'Five of us came to see the same play when I was thirteen,' reminded Bella.

'It was a lovely family weekend. All three of you loved the Natural History Museum more than anything,' said Elizabeth.

'And the science museum next door,' remembered Bella.

The following day at the airport, after giving big hugs to both, wiping her own tears, Bella said, 'don't cry, Mum. We will talk on skype or via WhatsApp video every week. And both of you can come for a holiday with us in Australia next year. We will definitely be back home for your 50th anniversary in the year after next.'

After saying goodbye to them, Elizabeth and Bella, both in tears, Julian drove back towards their home, only a couple of hours drive. On the way, Elizabeth said we must stop at the supermarket before getting home.

'Bella and Millie are coming home for the weekend. I think Richard is working and cannot come. It will be lovely to see the girls together after a long time. Three of us might go on a shopping spree,' Elizabeth said, humming to the music on the car radio.

Back home, Julian soon arranged to buy and fit safety Knobs for the gas stove and Gas Stove Alarms in the kitchen. He also removed the stack of their kitchen knives, keeping them in a high cupboard. He took over their cooking completely, often supplementing with takeaways. Elizabeth came down to the kitchen at times and just stood in front of the oven, looking amused.

At dinner time together, after Julian made a meal of their favourite dish one evening, Elizabeth commented, 'I am glad you liked the goulash. I made it exactly the way we had it the first time in that restaurant in Budapest. Luckily, you can find any recipe these days in the books.'

Julian tried to smile, sad with the memory of Budapest only five years back.

Julian managed to get a GP appointment for Elizabeth the same month. Their GP reviewed Elizabeth's medical history before asking about diet and alcohol.

'I am a teetotaller. This one likes his drink,' Elizabeth smiled, looking at Julian.

Then, the GP asked about any recent changes in her behaviour.

'I think I forget certain things lately. But we are all getting old. That is normal with age. Isn't it?' smiled Elizabeth at the GP.

The GP smiled back before asking if there was any history of memory problems in her family.

'Oh, I don't think so. My father died in his early sixties, and my mother passed away within two years,' Elizabeth replied quickly.

The GP then examined Elizabeth for her reflexes, coordination, muscle tone and strength, eye movement and speech.

'All normal, aren't they?' eagerly asked Elizabeth.

'Yes, they are all normal,' replied the GP

'I knew it,' said Elizabeth looking at Julian.

The GP told them, 'I am going to do a Mini-Mental State Exam test now. It takes longer than the Mini-Cog test but is more accurate. And we have the time.'

The GP asked questions like what the season was and the names of three objects, and to repeat them later, calculations like counting backwards, writing, and copying geometrical figures. Julian tried to concentrate on the gardening magazine on the table next to him.

After about ten minutes, the GP said to Elizabeth, 'we are all done now. Thanks.'

Both Julian and Elizabeth looked at the GP with questioning looks.

'The score was sixteen. I will need to refer you to the Memory Assessment Service at the hospital for further evaluation. I will request an MRI beforehand. It is better than a CT brain for this. I will also arrange some routine blood tests and an ECG in the meantime,' said the GP.

On the way home, Elizabeth talked about the big shopping they needed to do today while Julian drove silently. As a retired GP, he knew that a score of sixteen confirmed that Elizabeth had moderate dementia. And they did their 'big' shopping only yesterday.

It took almost three months before Elizabeth had her MRI of the brain. A few days later, the GP on the telephone confirmed to Julian that Elizabeth had Alzheimer's disease and not vascular dementia.

'This was what I thought with her history and when I examined her,' added the GP.

Six weeks later, the Memory Assessment Service in the hospital also confirmed this. While a Neuropsychiatrist was assessing Elizabeth, a support worker and an occupational therapist talked to Julian about future arrangements for Elizabeth at home.

At the end of the consultation, Julian asked the Neuropsychiatrist, 'what about Aricept or any similar drugs? I know the NICE UK recommends them.'

The Neuropsychiatrist said, 'we can prescribe them, but I am sure you know it can only reduce some of the symptoms of dementia. But they don't stop the progression of the disease. And sometimes they have side effects.'

'Let's give it a try anyway,' said Julian.

On the drive home, Elizabeth asked Julian, 'what did they say about you at the hospital? I cannot remember. I have been worried about you. But I am glad that you got properly checked up, though.'

Since his partial retirement, Julian has volunteered at their small town's Memory Café. Now once a week, he brought his wife Elizabeth there. Contacts with Age UK and the Alzheimer's Society gave him practical advice and support for caring for Elizabeth at home. Julian brought Elizabeth diligently for several weeks to the

Memory Matters sessions. But Elizabeth's memory loss progressed rapidly. Julian retired fully from his job with some sadness.

Over one weekend, their son Michael came with his wife and their children. Millie, now a second-year doctor hoping to become a cardiologist, also arrived. They had a family breakfast together. Then in the late morning, while Elizabeth was having a nap and the children watched TV, the whole family sat together to talk. Bella also joined on skype from Australia.

'Dad, you need support at home. It is too much for you. You are not getting any younger, you know,' said Michael.

'You already have Type 2 diabetes, blood pressure and high cholesterol,' added Millie.

'They are under control. I am also fully retired now and have all the time we need,' replied Julian.

'But everyone knows being a full-time carer for a person with memory loss is more than demanding. It is already taking a toll on you. Even from Skype calls, I can see you have lost weight,' said Bella.

'I am glad to have lost those extra pounds. My main concern with your Mum is that she sometimes comes down the stairs half asleep some nights. I am worried that she might slip and break her hip or something,' Julian said.

'Why don't you get a child safety gate for the stair? We had it for Bernie and now use the same thing for Tim. Although Tim never gets up at night,' said Emma.

Michael said, 'I will get one this afternoon from the shop in the town and fit it upstairs before I go.'

'Mummy, could we have some hot chocolate, please?' asked Bernie coming to them.

Emma went to the kitchen but came out soon and asked, 'is the microwave not working?'

'Sorry, the plug switch for the microwave is behind it on the wall. These days I always turn it off at the wall before leaving the kitchen,' replied Julian.

After further discussion, it was agreed that Julian and Elizabeth would have a home carer coming three times a week to clean.

'I will have more time to tidy up the garden then. As you see, it is in a mess now,' said Julian.

'I will do the lawn after lunch before I go this evening,' said Mille. 'But you have to pay me pocket money like before,' she smiled.

'All of five pounds for the week?' laughed Julian.

'No, it has gone up with the inflation,' smiled Millie.

Only Bella noticed on the laptop screen that Elizabeth was now behind them.

'Oh. When did you all come home? Lovely to see you all after a long time. How was the journey?' Elizabeth asked.

'It was fine,' both Michael and Millie replied.

'Hello. Mum,' said Bella on the Skype screen.

'Hello,' replied Elizabeth before turning to the rest of them and asking in a hushed voice, 'who is she?'

Trying to hide her tears, Bella said, 'goodnight. Love you all. It is after midnight here.'

Coming back home, where they grew up, has always been special to Michael, Mille and to Bella before she left for Australia. Michael's wife Emma also loved coming to this house with a large garden and open countryside as she grew up in a busy town. She often went for a walk with Elizabeth on the hill path with a fantastic view of the sea at a distance. Their children also loved visiting Nana and Grampa. They always looked forward to going for a walk with Nana and enjoyed watching her cook their favourite foods. On her eighth birthday, Nana helped Bernie to decorate the special cake with chocolate and icing. Since then, Bernie and Nana have made desserts for their dinner whenever they came over. The children loved both Nana and Grampa, but one could tell Nana was their favourite.

But now, while they still looked forward to coming over to their grandparents, Michael and Emma noticed that their attitude somehow stiffened when they were next to Elizabeth. Coming out of their car in their grandparents' driveway, Tim and Bernie ran toward Julian and Elizabeth as before but then froze before giving them a hug. They appeared confused when their Nana, at times, even ignored them. Michael and Emma had explained the situation best they could to Bernie, but Tim was too young. It made Michael even sadder.

One late afternoon, Bernie and Tim were playing in the garden. Emma was reading a book sitting on a chair outside, and enjoying the sun going down the hills. Julian, Michael, and Millie were watching TV in their living room while Elizabeth was still having her afternoon nap. Suddenly they heard shouting by the stairs. Elizabeth was coming down agitated.

'I need to get back home immediately. I will need to pick up Michael and Bella from school soon,' she said. 'Where are my car keys?' she was now almost shouting.

Julian came out with Michael and Mille to her and asked, 'what's the matter, darling?'

'We need to pick up the children from school. Let's go now. I don't like being late,' she replied.

'OK. I am ready. Let's go to the kitchen, and I will pick up the keys there,' Julian said calmly before guiding Elizabeth to the kitchen, holding her hand. There, he got a glass of water from the tap and gave it to Elizabeth, who had sat on one of the chairs by then. Then, after Elizabeth finished her drink, Julian held Elizabeth's hand. He said, 'Bernie and Tim want us to play with them in the garden. Shall we go?'

Elizabeth smiled and went to the garden and played with Bernie and Tim. They both cuddled her tightly.

Julian explained to Michael and Millie that they call this sundowning with dementia. 'Your Mum often in the evening, around dusk, gets very agitated. She starts shouting, arguing, pacing, or becoming even more confused about what's happening around her. As darkness falls and streetlights come on, she becomes increasingly concerned that she is in the wrong place or has forgotten to do something important.'

'You managed to calm her down quite easily,' said Millie.

'I have learnt to use distraction techniques like going into a different room, making her a drink, turning some music on, or going outside to the garden,' replied Julian.

'I know that caffeine and alcohol make sundowning worse. Now your Mum drinks only two cups of tea max any day. She never drank alcohol anyway. I have given up too.' Julian smiled with some sadness, adding, 'fortunately, this sundowning is not frequent with your Mum so far. And listening to our favourite music together is always soothing for both of us.'

It was becoming frequent lately that Elizabeth pushed Julian out of their bed. But Julian was still reluctant to sleep in another room, leaving her alone.

Then in the middle of one night, Elizabeth woke up and started shouting at Julian. 'Get away from me. Who are you? What are you doing in our bedroom at night?'

Julian tried to calm her down by saying, 'it's only me, darling. Your Jules. Come back to bed.'

Elizabeth continued shouting and said, 'I am going to dial 999 to call for the police,' and walked towards the landline phone in their room.

Julian had no choice but to leave the room. But when about fifteen minutes later, he came back to check upon Elizabeth, she was sitting upright on their bed, reading a book upside down. After seeing Julian, she said, 'hello, darling. What have you been doing downstairs? Watching a late-night movie again? Come to bed now. It's late.'

Added to these, Elizabeth started having frequent diarrhoea and vomiting. It became difficult to keep her clean even more than before. She also developed several rashes on her legs. As a GP, Julian knew of these side effects of the drug Elizabeth had been prescribed. He checked her pulse, which was now only fifty-five per minute compared to her usual seventy. Julian discussed and agreed with their regular GP that these looked like side effects of the drug Elizabeth was prescribed to control symptoms of her dementia. So, they decided to stop the medication, as the side effects were now more troublesome to manage, and there were no improvements in her dementia symptoms. Elizabeth's diarrhoea, vomiting and rash improved within a week, but her dementia progressed rapidly.

In the next few months, it was becoming impossible to care for Elizabeth at home even with daily support from care workers, weekly mental health nurse's visits, social care support, and Michael and Millie coming down most weekends.

Then, one morning, they had to call an ambulance for Julian with severe chest pain. Luckily, Michael was there with his wife and the children for a few days. Julian was told it was severe angina with a mild heart attack at the hospital. Coronary angiography was done urgently, showing a blocked blood vessel, and a stent was placed.

Upon hearing the news, Millie immediately came to the hospital, asking her colleagues to cover her own duty in her own hospital.

'I am so relieved that it was only a single vessel disease and could be stented,' said Mille to Julian, sitting by his bed. 'I heard that they will possibly discharge you the day after tomorrow. I will take the week off and stay with you,' she added, holding his hand.

Millie brought Julian home from the hospital two days later.

'Where the two of you have you been? Did you forget we were going out together to the country pub for dinner? Get ready quickly,' said Elizabeth as they arrived.

Julian was feeling almost back to normal in a couple of days. Emma had to go back with Bernie and Tim as Bernie was missing her school. Michael stayed for the week. One day, after Michael made lunch for the four of them, Elizabeth went for a nap upstairs.

The three of them stayed sat for a while.

'I am sorry, but the time has come for Mum to be looked after in a care home. That will be safe for both of you,' Millie insisted.

Michael said, 'we all know it is going to be tough for you to send her to a care home, but we really don't have another choice.'

A Skype phone call came through on Julian's iPad from Bella.

'I am so relieved that you are feeling better. Millie said it was one vessel only, and the results should be good,' said Bella. Then she echoed Millie and Michael's suggestion of arranging a care home for their mother.

'Alright, I will try to find a care home not far from here so I can visit her daily. But I would wait until our 39th wedding anniversary next month,' agreed Julian.

They all turned to find Elizabeth standing by the door. She said, 'are you coming to bed now, darling? Your friends have their home to go to as well.' Then she looked at the kitchen clock showing one-forty-five and said, 'look, it is way past midnight.'

It took some searching, but Julian found a care home only five miles from their house. The place had a good reputation amongst his GP colleagues in caring for people with dementia. One weekend when Millie was home, Julian went with her to check the place. It seemed clean and the rooms bright with all the necessary facilities. The care staff seemed pleasant and friendly with the fifteen or so people there with dementia. Julian booked the place for Elizabeth from the week after their anniversary.

Their 49th anniversary was in the middle of the week, and only Michael and Millie could come. Emma had to stay home as Bernie had to go to school. Millie had already brought a cake from M&S on her way.

While Michael Skyped Bella in Australia, everyone gathered by the kitchen table by lunchtime. Elizabeth had decided to put on her best dress which she had not worn for quite a while, and looking at Julian, she said, 'come on, darling. Put on something decent. It is our anniversary.' Then looking at the Skype screen, she said, 'Hello, darling. How is life in Australia? How is Richard? What time is it there now?'

They all tried to hold back their tears while Elizabeth insisted on cutting the cake. 'You are missing a lovely cake, darling. It's passion fruit and pistachio, your favourite,' she said to Bella on the screen.

'I am missing it already, Mum. Maybe, next year when I come home for your 50th. I have some good news for you all,' she said, then pointed to her tummy.

Millie asked excitedly, 'how many weeks now, Bell?'

'Eight weeks,' Bella replied.

But by then, Elizabeth was already slumped in a chair. Julian went to her and asked if she wanted a cup of tea or only cold water with her cake.

Elizabeth said, 'what cake? Who are these two people in our house? Did you invite them?'

Two weeks later, Elizabeth was transferred to the care home. Julian went to her late morning every day. Millie, Michael and occasionally Emma visited her whenever they could come down. But Bernie and Tim were never brought there – it was decided it would be too traumatic for them. Both often asked about their Nana and were told she was not well and being looked after in a special place.

'When is she going to be back?' Bernie asked sometimes.

Michael and Emma were always honest with their children and simply said, 'we don't know.'

In the beginning, when Julian visited Elizabeth, according to the caring staff, she seemed to perk up a bit. The care staff said, apparently, she was in the habit of wandering around the place and sometimes getting into other residents' rooms. But lately, she seems to get upset easily. The staff did not tell Julian that Elizabeth had been throwing food and dinner plates at them and was verbally abusive. They did not also mention that she was found hoarding some of her breakfast and dinner in her drawers.

Over the next few months, during his daily visits, Julian noticed Elizabeth was becoming sleepier. At times she slept peacefully under a blanket for the whole period of Julian's visit in the late morning. But when she woke up, seeing Julian next to her, she always smiled and occasionally said, 'hello darling. I am up now and going to make our breakfast. What do you want today?' Then she would hold Julian's hand tightly and again fall asleep peacefully.

But soon, it became more traumatic for Julian when Elizabeth did not recognise him at all and, at times, became so agitated that he had to leave. Michael and Millie have been facing the same issue with Mum almost from when she went to the care home. But the family found it hard to share this anguish with each other. Julian, however, continued his daily visits to Elizabeth, hail or storm, just to see the face he had been in love with for over fifty years. Rare cognition of his presence on Elizabeth's face kept him going. He was suffering from depression but did his best to hide from his children. The news of the birth of another granddaughter from Australia made him even sadder that he could not share this with Elizabeth.

Until two years back, Christmas was always at Mum and Dad's. Everyone came, and Elizabeth cooked her famous Christmas turkey with her special chestnut stuffing. Bella and Millie helped, lately joined by Emma and Bernie, while Michael and Julian tidied up the place and set the table.

But this year, only Millie came to visit Elizabeth with Julian on Christmas day. Elizabeth slept peacefully all the time they sat by her. Bella rang from Australia on Julian's videophone to share her two-week-old daughter's face with Mum on Christmas day, to no avail. Neither Julian nor Millie and Bella could hide their tears this time.

January 2020 was bitterly cold as usual, but Julian visited Elizabeth daily, mostly sitting by her when she slept. But on the rare occasion when she was up, he sensed a hint of a smile as he said hello. Michael and Millie have been very busy with their work and could visit only once during the month. From Australia, Bella said they were planning to come over with their baby Liliana in the spring. She did not have the heart to say they were coming for her parents' 50th as she had promised.

After February had been one of the wettest on record, the spring had more sunshine than one saw in most summers. On a sunny day, Julian picked up some daffodils from their garden. He remembered Elizabeth had planted the bulbs there only three years back while he was busy mowing the lawn on a lovely autumn afternoon.

Soon the TV channels were full of news of the new virus they called Covid, spreading everywhere, even in the UK. Most of the time, Julian switched off the TV and flicked through many albums they had of their days from wedding and their children growing up. He wished he could share those unforgettable memories with Elizabeth for one more time.

Millie sounded exhausted whenever she could find time to call Julian. She said she was scared because the hospital was becoming overwhelmed with Covid, and most of the time, they had no protective equipment.

'Be very careful, Dad,' she said and added that she would not be visiting Mum for the time being to avoid bringing the infection to her from the hospital.

Their friend Barry telephoned in the second week of March early in the morning, sounding extremely distraught. Beverly was taken to hospital the night before by an ambulance after a fall down the stairs. She was having emergency surgery for her broken hip. Julian went to comfort Barry at home before taking him to the hospital during the late afternoon visiting time the same day. They sat by her bed while Beverly slept.

The nurses, all wearing masks and plastic aprons, said she was given strong painkiller injections. A man came wearing something like a spacesuit and introduced himself as the anaesthetist. After checking Beverly, he said to the two of them, 'the operation went well. She seems to be doing well. My colleague, the surgeon, is busy with another case. We have a load to do today.'

After a while, Julian took Barry to the hospital canteen for a cup of tea. When they returned to her bedside, Beverly was still sleeping. There appeared to be some uneasy atmosphere amongst the staff everywhere in the hospital, with much whispering.

Later, Julian drove Barry back. On the way, he went to the busy supermarket to buy some microwave dinner for the two to take home. The store was exceptionally busy for a midweek evening. People were filling up their trollies, and many shelves were empty. Some were talking openly about the impending lockdown to tackle Covid.

A few days later, Michael telephoned. 'Hi, Dad. How are you? How is Mum?'

'I have a bit of a cold since this morning, not too bad. Mum is OK – she smiled at me yesterday. How are Bernie and Tim? Have not seen them for a while. How is Emma doing in her new job, and how are you?'

'We are all fine here, thanks. Please be very careful with this new Covid thing, Dad.'

'I don't go out these days except to see your Mum. Don't worry.'

When Julian visited Elizabeth in the care home later in the morning, two ambulances were parked in the front. From one of the ambulances, two men wearing spacesuit-like outfits pushed a patient from the ambulance to the care home on a trolley.

Everyone inside the care home seemed to be in a hurry.

One of the care workers Julian knew well said, 'all the rooms in the care home are filled up now. They were going to convert the sitting area into a four-bedded room like in the hospital. We had so many people transferred from the hospital with very little notice. Some of the staff here have got Covid and are now in hospital. We don't have enough staff and don't know how we would manage.'

Julian felt happy that Elizabeth briefly smiled at him again after he arrived. However, he could not stay for very long as he was feeling miserable with headaches and body aches. Back home, Julian went straight to bed with a dry cough. But he had to get up soon. To his surprise, he found it difficult to breathe lying flat. He propped himself with pillows and started watching TV, now full of news about Covid. The GP in him told him it might be the Covid symptoms he was having. Still, Julian tried to assure himself that it was a simple lousy cold. He took a few more paracetamols and fell asleep completely exhausted.

In the evening, Millie telephoned. But she immediately called an ambulance for Julian after hearing him on the phone, almost gasping for breath. The ambulance arrived nearly two hours later and had to push open the front door. Julian was in a desperate situation, with his oxygen saturation only seventy per cent. He was rushed to the makeshift ICU in the operation theatre recovery area at the hospital.

Millie called one of her college friends at the hospital where Julian was admitted and learned he was being ventilated. She had earlier telephoned Michael about Dad's situation. Millie only said to him now, 'he is stable in ICU now and having the best possible care.'

'I am so worried. And now, they are not allowing relatives to visit patients in the hospital. I want to go and see him so much,' replied Michael.

'I will try to go there tomorrow after I finish my night shift tonight. I will sneak in with my hospital badge and talk to the ICU team. Listen, I must go now. It is hectic here, and I have also to try to find time to speak to Bella in Australia.'

The following day Michael tried to call the nursing home to find out about Mum without luck. He kept trying, and after about an hour, the reception desk told him they were very busy. Many staff were off sick, and now the care home was utterly full of sick patients. But Michael was reassured that Elizabeth was well. He immediately sent a text to Millie and Bella with the news.

During the morning handover at the hospital, Millie found that her colleague for the day has fallen ill with Covid. She was asked to cover until 5 pm. While grabbing breakfast at the canteen, she texted her friend to find out about Julian in the other hospital. She was assured later that Julian was stable on a ventilator and relayed the news to Michael and Bella.

After finishing her shift, Millie went home for a shower first. She had planned to drive to the hospital where Julian was admitted, only an hour and a half away. But the exhaustion of working two shifts took over, and she fell asleep.

The next morning, from work, Millie texted her friend at Julian's hospital only to find that she was off sick. Luckily, the staff looking after Julian answered her call to the ICU. She assured Millie that Julian, though critical, was stable. During her brief lunch break, Millie called Elizabeth's nursing home two hours later. After only a couple of attempts, the receptionist answered to say Elizabeth had taken ill with Covid.

'Which hospital are they transferring Mum to?' Millie asked. The receptionist said that because of Elizabeth's dementia, she would not be considered for transfer to hospital care. Millie asked to speak to the care home manager, but the receptionist disconnected the call after a few seconds. Devastated, Millie texted Michael and Bella.

Millie managed to sneak into Julian's hospital the next day but could only see him from a distance on a ventilator with tubes sticking out of him everywhere. She was told they were struggling to keep him going. Neither Michael nor Millie was allowed to visit Elizabeth in the nursing home.

The following day, Millie got a call that Julian had passed away. Elizabeth's nursing home called only an hour later to say she had passed away.

Three days later, on Tuesday, 7th April, Elizabeth and Julian were buried in graves next to each other in their local cemetery. It would have been their 50th anniversary on this day. Only Millie and Michael could attend, keeping their distance from each other.

They wanted to hug each other, but it was not advisable.

In another life

Today, 1st December 2017, I would have been in the tropical jungle of Costa Rica with a view of the beautiful Arenal Volcano if I had flown there last Sunday.

But I did not fly last Sunday.

For the last three weeks, I have been having headaches. In the beginning, a couple of paracetamols two or three times a day was enough to keep it under control, and I got on with my usual routines. Daytime volunteering in the community and badminton on two evenings had gone on as usual. But my badminton was getting slightly worse, which I only noticed. I had put it down to old age. After all, I was over seventy years old.

But in the last week, my headache intensified. Paracetamol and Ibuprofen, together several times a day, were not enough now. But I braved on and even went last week to play my last night of badminton before going on holiday.

Not only was I ashamed of my poor coordination, but even my friends on the court have also said, 'you look tired out. You definitely need a holiday.'

The next day, Saturday, I got myself ready for my early Sunday morning departure for my holiday, stuffing myself with all sorts of painkillers. I have made sure to pack enough of them in my rucksack. But when my daughter came to say goodbye to me in the late afternoon, after only one look at the way I was moving, she had taken me to the hospital. By then, even for getting into and out of her car, I needed her to hold on to me to stop me from toppling over. An emergency CT scan at the hospital showed a large amount of blood clots pressing on both sides of my brain.

The neurosurgeon came to talk to me about emergency surgery to cut open my skull. Realising that I was a surgeon, he said, 'we have no choice but to operate as soon as possible. Obviously, you understand the possible outcomes. There is a chance that you may recover fully, but also possible that you may end up with severe disabilities. And there is also a small chance that you might not make it.'

I nodded and signed the consent form with a shaky hand. I said, 'no CPR in case of cardiac arrest.' My daughter explained that I had instructed her on this for some time. I had to sign another form.

December 2017

I wake up to hear a couple of doctors and a nurse talking by my bedside. I try to say something, but only saliva dribbles out of my mouth. The nurse comes and uses a tube to suck the spit out of my mouth and throat. They talk about speaking to my relatives as soon as possible. I drift off.

I open my eyes to see a nurse next to me. She says, 'I am Linda, ICU Sister. We are going to clean you now. Being Saturday, we don't know when the Consultant Anaesthetist will do her rounds.'

I try to speak, but nothing comes out. I think I must have been here for the whole week if it was Saturday.

The consultant arrives later with a couple of juniors. After examining my charts and then myself, she tells me, 'soon, we will be transferring you to the ward. Maybe tomorrow.' Then looking at the nurses, she says, 'best to put a proper feeding tube and a Silastic catheter today. Also, please ask the physiotherapist to talk to me.'

As she turns to leave, I hear the voice of the neurosurgeon who talked to me before my surgery.

'I did not know you were on call this weekend,' I hear the anaesthetist says to him. Then ignoring me, they talk to each other for a while.

I can only hear bits of their conversation. 'it was touch and go.' -------- 'Well, he is at least off the ventilator now' ---- 'He had told his daughter sometime back he does not want CPR in case of an arrest.' ----- 'I must go now – they are waiting for me in the theatre.'

Then they all disappear. I drift off.

The next thing I notice through the corner of my eyes is my daughter sitting by my bed with the sorriest face I had ever seen since our wonderful dog Digger died when she was twelve. Seeing me awake, she gets up and holds my hand. I can just about feel her touch but cannot squeeze her hand. Tears flood her eyes – she was always the emotional one growing up. Then, trying to bring a smile to her face, she asks, 'how are you feeling today?' Tears drop on her cheeks.

I say, 'don't cry. I will be OK.' But nothing comes out of my mouth, only some dribble of saliva. I wish she was not crying. I wish I could give her a hug. A few tears roll down my cheeks. She gets some tissue to wipe off my tears and then my dribble. Then she wipes her own tears. After a while, she leaves after giving me a light hug.

Soon two people with jolly faces come and introduce themselves as physiotherapists. They move my flaccid arms and legs a few times before they leave. I drift off.

I can see my bed being pushed over the hospital as the bland roof of the corridor moves above me. Then it stops before going inside a small place and then going down. I realise we are on a lift. The voice says, 'second floor,' and they push me again for a while.

'I am the sister here. Welcome,' someone says.

Days go by. Nurses do everything for me. Physios come daily. I wish I could say 'thank you to them,' but only dribbles come out of my mouth.

Then one day, someone comes and introduces herself as the speech therapist. She teaches me to blink once for 'yes' and twice for 'no.' She returns in a couple of days with some flashcards. Small words are written in them with pictures like 'yes' with a smiley face and 'no' with a grumpy face. After spending some time with me, she leaves, saying, 'I am leaving these cards in your locker. I will tell the nurses to use them and your family too when they visit you.'

I want to say thank you but don't know how to without someone holding the cards for me.

A neurologist comes and examines me one day for a while before saying, 'I understand you were a surgeon yourself. I will be open and honest with you. As far as we can see, you have complete quadriplegia and aphasia. I think the aphasia may be temporary, but we must wait and see. In the meantime, we will get an MRI scan done and let us continue with the physio and the speech therapist.'

I want to ask him more, but nothing comes out of my mouth. I only blink once, and he leaves.

My daughter comes every evening looking shattered. Sometimes my son-in-law comes too, but never my grandchildren. After seeing my flashcards, my son-in-law says, 'I think there is an app one can get for people who benefit from symbol and photo support. I will check.'

I just look at him.

Another day, my daughter brings some colourful Christmas cards made by my grandchildren for me and holds them in front of me. I try to smile, but only tears flood my eyes. I so wish I could see their lovely faces. Her eyes are also full of tears. Soon she leaves.

The physios come in pairs twice daily and spend a long time with me. The nurse tells me the speech therapist is on leave and she would not be coming until after Christmas.

Suddenly a word comes out of my mouth. I utter, 'thhhan uu.' The nurse smiles and says, 'fantastic. You are beginning to speak now.' I smile at her.

The next day when my daughter comes and says hello to me, I reply, 'hhellllo.' Smile and tears flood her eyes.

Words bubble out of my mouth in the next few days, although I cannot yet speak most words or a full sentence.

The neurologist returns after my MRI scan while my daughter is also there. He explains, 'from the MRI, it looks like you will have to learn to live with paralysis of all four limbs. We will arrange for you to have a gastrostomy rather than use the nasogastric tube for your feeding. I will refer to one of the surgeons for this. I hope they can fit you in soon. Then we have to think of transferring to a proper care home.'

I say, 'thaannh uu,' before he leaves.

I can hear some people singing Christmas carols one day when all the nurses and physios had come with some glitters around their heads and necks. They say, 'Merry Christmas' to each other but avoids me. My daughter comes and sits next to me for a while, trying to hide her tears. I want to tell her to go home and spend time with my granddaughters but can only look at her and say, 'ggo hhommme.' After a while, she leaves, giving me a kiss on my cheek. The nurses come and give me a sponge wash while talking to themselves about their husband or partner making the Christmas dinner this year.

I hear the nurses laughing and joking about their Christmas with family for the next few days. My daughter talks about how my granddaughters had more fun hiding in large cardboard boxes than with all their new toys. I surprise her by saying, 'mmmy lluvv ttooo thhemm.'

In a few days, they wheel me to the operation theatre and put me to sleep. I wake up with that irritating tube gone from my nose.

My daughter comes in the evening and says, 'great that you had the gastrostomy done now.' Then she explains she would be on call for the next few days and wouldn't be able to visit. Some of her colleagues are off sick. 'When I come next time, I will tell you about the care home we are thinking of you taking to.'

'I say, 'nno wworrry. Ggo hhooomme.'

December 2017

I wake up to hear a couple of doctors and a nurse talking by my bedside. I mutter, 'good morning.'

They come next to me, and one says, 'good evening. How are you feeling?'

I point to my head and say, 'bit sore there.'

The nurse soon brings over some injections, and I fall asleep again.

My daughter is sitting by the bedside. Seeing me open my eyes, she smiles. 'How are you feeling today?'

'Only a bit sore over the stitches. Not too bad. Could you please make the bed upright so that I can sit up?'

She and a nurse sit me up. Then my daughter gives me two cards my twin granddaughters had made for me. She tells me that she had already emailed my family in India and friends that my operation has gone well.

The neurosurgeon, with his team, comes for his ward round soon. He smiles at me and says, 'you are a lucky man. There was a lot of blood pressing on both sides of your brain. But you should be fine.'

'Thanks very much to you and your team. When do you think I can go home? When can I drive, and when can I fly again? I was due to go to volunteer in Rajasthan in six weeks,' I ask in a hurry.

'Well, home probably the day after tomorrow. Driving after about six weeks. And hopefully, you should be OK to fly after about 2-3 months. I will see you the day after tomorrow.'

'By the way, we found you have Type 2 diabetes. A dietician will come and talk to you soon,' says one of the junior doctors coming back later.

The nurse brings over some lunch on a tray, Shepard's pie with green peas. I eat quickly –

must have been hungry. Soon my daughter gets up to leave.

'Could you please bring my iPad and phone when you come next time?' I ask.

In the afternoon, two physiotherapists come over. First, they ask me to move my arms and legs and then help me stand up. Then, I walk a few steps carefully, holding their hands.

The following morning, the night nurses remove my catheter. Later, I walk by myself with one of the nurses by my side to the toilet.

'I will wait outside. Don't close the door,' she says.

After my lunch, I have a nap. When I wake up, I see my daughter sitting next to me with my son-in-law.

'How are you doing? Home tomorrow,' they say. My daughter gives me my iPad.

'Are you sure you don't want to come and stay with us for a couple of weeks?' they ask.

'No thanks. You will both have work to go to anyway, and the twins will be with the childminder. It will be easier for me to manage in my own small single bedroom ground floor flat. But thanks anyway.'

'I have made some meals you like and will put them in your fridge. I will get some milk, bread, and bananas later. Do you want me to get anything you fancy?' my daughter asks.

They leave soon, and I open my iPad. Many emails and messages from my friends and family. I leave them alone for now and send an email to the Charity hospital in Rajasthan, where I was due to be volunteering in six weeks. I ask them that we have to postpone this by three months. Then I send emails to my town's Foodbank and the Community Caring group that I would not be able to join them for at least another month. I cannot keep my eyes open any longer and drift off.

The next morning after breakfast, I walk again by myself along the long corridor of the ward a few times. Then after the late morning tea and snacks, I talk to the patient in the next bed who had his operation on the same day as me.

He was 43 years old, tall, and athletically built. He had been a keen cyclist, a regular swimmer and loved football. Ten days back, he took his wife and their young children to the town in the evening to show them Christmas light decorations. And probably do some early Christmas shopping, not the Santa presents, of course, they will have to be done without the children around. While the children were mesmerised by the lights, he had an epileptic fit and became unconscious for a while. He was brought to the hospital by ambulance. A scan showed a brain tumour, and he had an operation. He will also be going home tomorrow, the 5th day of the Christmas month.

Later, sitting on my bed, I try to imagine that his children would happily talk about their house's Christmas decorations with their Daddy back home. They will keep reminding him that they have been 'very good' this year and hope Santa will bring them all the presents they have already written for. They will chatter about fun things they are doing at school, and he will definitely come to their Christmas play. They will have the best Christmas ever in their life with their dad. He will make sure of that. Because even with the best treatment available, he will start going downhill soon. He has already lost his vision in one eye!

His family and children will have him for three or four Christmas at best.

I feel lucky and a bit guilty at the same time.

The following day, my daughter drives me back to my flat. The first thing I do is to turn on my TV to watch some cricket on the screen while she makes some tea for us. Later in the afternoon, they bring over my twin granddaughters. Usually, they jump to my lap immediately. But this time, they are a bit shy/scared seeing the prominent scars with stitches on my head.

Soon, I tell them a story that some butterfly had laid eggs inside my head. It had turned into three cocoons, and they had to make three holes in my head to let them out. Once they cut it open, to everyone's surprise, three beautiful butterflies flew out of my head. Only three years old, they are a bit sceptical at first but soon get back to chatting with me and start playing with their toys on my lap.

After they leave, I put the shepherd's pie my daughter had made in the microwave. Later, I have a body shower and rub a wet towel on my head and face avoiding the stitches. In the mirror, I can see they had used clips to close the wounds on my head – looks impressive. I am totally knackered soon and fall asleep in my own bed.

The next day after breakfast, I decide to take a walk outside my flat. Covering my head with a woolly hat, I walk to the town only 500m away. After about 100m, I chastise myself for being stupid to walk so far and back on my own after such a major operation and come back home. After having a cup of tea, I Skype my family in India. They are shocked to see my scars, delighted to see me so well, and repeatedly ask me to take it easy. My only sister says that she wished she could come and visit me and take care of me but knows that's impossible. I assure her I am doing well and maybe even visiting India in a few months.

In the next few days, I walk further and even one day visit my colleagues in the Foodbank Charity and, one evening, my badminton club. They are all surprised and happy to see me doing so well. Back at my flat, I wish I could do something more – I seem full of energy. This is in spite of sleeping only three to four hours at night. Then while taking my prescribed medicine, I find the answer. I have been prescribed steroids to reduce the swelling of my brain. It's the steroid talking – not me fully rejuvenated – I must be careful not to overdo things. I order the TV channel offering viewing of the Ashes test series in Australia, played mostly at night-time in the UK.

I also order online Christmas presents for my daughter's family in the next few days. And gradually, I increase my walking down to the town, now with Christmas decorations everywhere and back.

On Christmas day, my son-in-law takes me to their house in the late morning. My daughter is busy cooking. Excitedly, my grandchildren show me their Christmas tree decorations and their presents. Then they bring out the gifts for me from them before opening their presents from me under the trees and giving me hugs and kisses. I try to hide my tears.

While I sit on a sofa, they come and check my scar on the head, now without clips. They ask if really there were butterflies in my head. I repeat the story. They look at my daughter, who only smiles. They go to play with their new toys. Soon, we have our Christmas dinner wearing our party hats. I enjoy my daughter's roast potato and gravy more than anything. After dinner, I feel exhausted, and my daughter brings me back to my flat.

In the next few days, I walk more every day and feel good enough to start a normal life again. But I decide to give myself a few more weeks. My daughter or my son-in-law brings over my granddaughters for a few hours on some days. I watch them play happily and then tell them make-up stories on my lap.

2018 New Year

I can hear everyone wishing a happy new year to each other today. My daughter and son-in-law come in the afternoon.

I surprise them by saying, 'Aaappy Nnuyeer. Hhow aarre u?' I want to ask them about my granddaughters, but words fail me.

My daughter shows me pictures of them playing with their new toys on her iPad. My son-in-law, an engineer, says, 'we are going to get you a voice-activated computer screen laptop.' He explains that it will have an Infrared/Sound/Touch Switch. I would be able to operate it with virtually any kind of body motion – even the blink of an eye or any other muscles of my face.

I ask, 'hhooww mmuuchh?'

They say, 'don't worry about it. And it's only less than five hundred quids.' Then they talk about Dame Hannah Care Home in my town. They have been discussing with them my transfer there, hopefully in the next few weeks.

I say, 'tthaankk uu,' but wish I could go back to my flat.

The speech therapist comes back in the first week of January.

'Sorry, I have been away for a while. You seem to have made good progress already.' Then she goes through her session with me and promises to return at least every week. I have a craving for some sweets to suck. The speech therapist asks the nurse.

She replies, 'you are not allowed sweets, even to suck. They found you have Type 2 diabetes the day after the operation.'

I only can say, 'Ohhh!'

'They probably did not tell you because you have all your feed through the gastrostomy tube.' Then she leaves.

After the next couple of days, my daughter and son-in-law arrive with smiles on their faces.

'We think we have found the right voice-activated screen laptop for you. We wanted to show you on my iPad before we order it,' my son-in-law says enthusiastically.

I reply, 'I am tired,' and close my eyes.

Next, I hear whispers near my bed. A nurse had cleaned my ears only the day before. One of the nurses was telling my daughter softly, 'he has been very depressed for the last few days. They have made a psychiatric referral.'

My daughter comes over to me and, holding my hand, says, 'we have to go now. I will try to come back the day after tomorrow.'

A nurse comes later to give my face a wipe. I tell her to go away by shaking my head and close my eyes. I do the same next day to the speech therapist and then to someone who introduces himself as the psychiatrist.

When my daughter comes next time, alone, I say, 'oottherr ddayy ssoorry.'

She holds my hand and gives it a squeeze. Then she shows videos of my granddaughters dancing making me smile.

2018 New year

Now four weeks since my op, and I feel great even though the steroids have now been tailed off. My grandchildren come over with their parents in the New Year. Soon we go for a drive and then a short walk by the Moor and have a picnic. Wonderful few hours.

Back at my flat, while my daughter makes tea, my granddaughters rub their fingers gently on the pits on my skull, now almost healed. They ask me if really some butterflies came out of my head. I repeat the story, and satisfied, they get busy with their hot chocolate.

After they go home, I open my laptop. The first thing I do is to let the Charity Hospital in

Rajasthan know that I will be going over there in late March if that suits them and the rest of the team.

Then I search the website for a Voyage to the North Pole. I have already been to Antarctica, and now I want to fulfil another of my dream. I find that you could travel to the North Pole in three ways. Helicopter ride from Svalbard, an archipelago between mainland Norway and the North Pole. Either directly to the North Pole 1000km away or a helicopter ride 80km south of the North Pole and then ski from there to the pole.

I chose the third way, sailing 2341 km by a nuclear-powered icebreaker ship. Only between July and August, a maximum of five tours like these take place starting from Murmansk in northern Russia. It only takes about 124 passengers and had two dozen expedition team members and 140 crew.

I ring my daughter. When she answers, a bit worried, 'what's up? Is everything alright?'

I say, 'I am going to the North Pole this summer.'

She is stunned but has known me all her life and just laughs.

Six weeks to the day since my op, I go to the local Foodbank and start working for a few hours. The next day I start driving a few miles around the town at the quiet time of the day. After a few days, I ring up the Community Care team and say that I am now ready to go back to meet and spend time with people with disability as before.

One of the persons I was spending time with before has severe dementia. He does not even notice that I had been away for a few weeks, nor does he comment on the shallow pits on my head. The other person with a mental health issue I visit asks me about my head. But he is easily satisfied when I simply say that I had an operation there. The same week in the evenings, I return to my two badminton clubs. They are all happy and surprised to see me. I play only one game each evening – I must start slowly and build it up, not overdo it, I remind myself.

My grandchildren often come to stay with me and play. I read picture books with them, but they love my make-up stories more. Occasionally, I pick them up from their nursery school before taking them to the park. I feel back to my normal, if not 100%, at least 95%.

Before booking my flights to Rajasthan, I phone the only other surgeon in our volunteering team. I explain that since this will be my first flight and operating after my brain op, he must be there and ready for any eventuality. He sounds more than supportive. While I go back full swing to my community and Foodbank work, I limit my badminton to a minimum. I don't want to take any chance just yet.

2018 Spring

In the last three months, with the help of my speech therapist, my oral communication is now back to almost normal. Recently my daughter and son-in-law brought a brand-new voice-activated laptop. My son-in-law has also put all the files from my old laptop at home on this new one. Only a few years back, while I was working in Australia, I scanned and filed all the old photographs on my old laptop.

Now, I spend most of my time looking at those photos of the places I had travelled to, almost sixty countries and seven continents. The only problem is I have to shout to get one of the nurses to turn on the laptop. But looking at the family photographs is more unique. While I enjoy the memories of my family in India, where I was born and grew up, browsing through the photos of my own family sometimes brings tears to my eyes. I look at the pictures of my first daughter again and again. I try to remember the joy she brought to my life until five years back today when she suddenly passed away. She was not even thirty-two!

I have assessment after bloody assessment almost every other week. They still cannot find a suitable care home in the whole county that will take an over seventy-year-old man with paralysis of all four limbs. Working in the NHS hospitals for over thirty-five years, I know about the shortage of beds in hospitals. I wish I could die, and they could give this bed to someone else. Maybe because I am depressed, but somehow, I sense a 'not him again' in the eyes of the senior nurses and managers. So much I wish euthanasia was lawful in this country.

The speech therapist notices that I speak clearly now and don't dribble. With another colleague helping, she gives me a bedside swallow test. At first, they carefully examine my lips, teeth, and tongue. Then they check my cheeks and soft palate before asking me to smack my lips together and then sticking out my jaw. Next, they ask me to make sounds like coughing and clearing my throat. They use a tongue blade and gently push down my tongue firmly, confirming my gagging and coughing reflexes. Finally, I pass in all the tests. They allow me to have my first oral drinks for months with a straw. Wonderful.

But I am frustrated that I still have to shout for someone to turn on my laptop.

Over the weekend, when my daughter arrives after more than two weeks, the first thing she says is, 'I am sorry I could not come last week. I was on call. It was extremely busy.' Then she watches the smile on my face and asks, 'what has been happening? Anything new? Have they found a place for you?'

The nurse comes with a straw, and I sip from a cup she holds. 'We have started him on liquids orally for him since last week and hopefully will start on proper semisolid food from tomorrow. They are thinking of removing the gastrostomy tube the week after if everything goes well,' she says as I finish my drink.

The hospital has got a special chair for me now. Almost every other day, the physios strap me to that and wheel me around the hospital corridors. My daughter sometimes joins the two physios taking me out of the building to a small garden next to a massive car park on sunny days. For the first time in months, I view the open blue sky with a few soft clouds gently drifting by.

In the next few months, the news channels on my laptop are full of rightist groups 'Go back home' chants and violence. This has been getting worse since the Brexit referendum, only two years back.

With nothing else to do, I decide to start writing a book for the first time in my life. English was my second language, and I know it is audacity, especially as my grammar skills are poor. I start searching online about British Colonial history, especially in its crown jewel India. Some of the information I learn for the first time is horrifying. I start writing the book as historical fiction of a collection of short stories spanning four centuries, from the early seventeenth century till Brexit. I try to write it from the perspectives of the Indian immigrants settling in the country. It keeps me busy anyway.

My daughter when she finds time to come. She and the nurses, at times, tell me now that I can feed orally, the chance of finding a care home should be better. But nothing comes up. It may be my paranoia, but I feel like a piece of unwanted furniture in the living room, clogging up space in the already crowded place. Sometimes my daughter sends me videos on my laptop of my grandchildren playing or doing naughty things. They look so much grown up. So much I wish I could see them, but I understand that it will be too traumatic for them.

2018 Spring

Almost three months to the day I was discharged from the hospital, in early March, I arrive at Heathrow Airport. Once inside the terminal, the buzz of travelling around the world takes over me as before. I had chosen business class comfort this time just to be safe for the long flight. The change of flight from Delhi to Jodhpur and then a long car ride to the charity hospital went without a hitch. I work and operate at the hospital as I had always done for the whole week. My colleagues are pleasantly surprised and often say so.

Back home after almost two weeks, I immediately check for further international volunteering opportunities in the autumn. There is a call for another surgeon to join working with a team in The

Gambia in early November. I confirm my availability, but there will be a few months' gaps between my return from the North Pole trip and this.

Life is too short! Then I think I had never been to South Africa, although I have travelled to many parts of the continent. The whale watching season there is between August and October. I book a tour in September to Hermanus on the southern coast and include Kruger National Park and Cape Town in my itinerary.

The next three months are returning to my previous normal, and eagerly awaiting the North Pole trip. The TV and radio channels are full of rightist groups 'Go back home' chants and violence. This has been getting worse since the Brexit referendum, only two years back. With plenty of time in hand, I decide to start writing a book for the first time in my life. English was my second language, and I know it is audacity, especially as my grammar skills are poor. I start searching British Colonial history, especially in its crown jewel India. Some of the information I learn for the first time is horrifying. I write the book as historical fiction of a collection of short stories spanning four centuries from the early seventeenth century till Brexit. I try to write it from the perspectives of the Indian immigrants settling in this country.

My grandchildren often come to my place and spend hours playing with their toys or going for a walk with me to the nearby park. They are growing up so quickly.

2018 Early Summer

Still waiting for a placement in a care home. My daughter is busy – she skypes me when she can and tries to come once a week. One day my son-in-law comes with my daughter and shows me the special mobility chair he has found online. I know that I will need one when they can transfer me to a care home. I ask the price and gulp when he says it's less than twenty-five thousand pounds. Then he shows me a model like which Professor Hawkins uses. It costs about two hundred and fifty thousand pounds, he adds.

'Absolutely no way. I don't have that amount of money in my savings anyway,' I reply.

Then my daughter timidly says they are going on holiday for a couple of weeks next week. I wish them a good time and ask them to take lots of pictures.

I have nearly finished writing the book. There is so much horrible history of colonialism I did not know about. It's a pity that so many books on the subject are only in print, and I cannot read them on my laptop. Now would be the time for revision and again, revision of my book. I have always hated revision during my student days. But it keeps me busy, along with learning how one can publish a book for the first time.

The news on my laptop is all about the coming football world cup. Only occasionally the staff drag me on my chair to the TV room by the ward. Most of the time, someone is watching serials there, Eastender or other TV series – of no interest to me. And if by any chance the World cup football is on, soon they drag me back to my bed as the time for their handover comes. But I don't regret that I refused to pay a hefty subscription for TV channels on my laptop when my son-in-law had asked earlier.

I have sent letters with my book description to a couple of dozens of literary agents. But it does not look like any traditional publisher or agent would be interested in an unknown first-time writer. I am neither a TV celebrity, a correspondent for The Times or another newspaper, nor a retired or discredited politician. I am not sure I want to go on pursuing that route anymore. And if by any chance they pick me, the book will not be published for at least another year. I definitely don't want to carry on living that long if I have a choice.

2018 Summer

I have nearly finished writing the book. There is so much horrible history of colonialism I did not know about. Now is the time for revision and again revision. I have always hated revision during my student days. But it is interesting learning ways how one can publish a book for the first time. Working in the community, playing badminton, watching cricket, and ensuing world cup football on the TV, plus the book, keep me busy.

The news channels are full of the football world cup. I look forward to going to Russia for the first time in my life when the World Cup will be on there. I have arranged to visit Moscow for a few days before flying to Murmansk for my North Pole

Voyage. I have no doubt Moscow will be joyous with the football going on, although I will not be going to any live football match.

I have sent letters with my book description to a couple of dozens of literary agents. But it does not look like any traditional publisher or agent would be interested in an unknown first-time writer. I am neither a TV celebrity, a correspondent for The Times or another newspaper, nor a retired or discredited politician. I am not sure I want to go on pursuing that route anymore. And if by any chance they pick me, the book will not be published for at least another year. I definitely don't want to wait that long.

Finally, I arrive in Moscow in July 2018. The city is beautiful. The avenues by the Kremlin, Red Square and Sparrow Hill area are buzzing with football fever, especially as Russia has reached the quarterfinals. After a few days there, I arrive at the small city of Murmansk by the Barents Sea.

Then the voyage on a massive nuclear power ice breaker towards the North Pole. Every year only around six hundred people reach the North Pole, less than the number who successfully climbed Mt Everest in 2017! I feel lucky to be one of them.

The North Pole is only 5000km away. After the first 1000km of the open sea, our nuclear-powered icebreaker gets busy breaking through packed ice for the rest of the voyage. The ship has a library, a gym, and a sauna. But what catches my eye is a badminton court where the Russian crews played. After watching them for a while, I ask if I could join. They motion me in, and we play doubles. This becomes my place for the rest of the tour if there is nothing to watch outside - good fun.

In the evening, with a few members of the expedition team, one from France, I watch France vs Belgium semi-final game. At half time, all the expedition crew leave. I think they had gone for an urgent briefing. Soon they return with many passengers carrying a birthday cake and candles and sing Happy Birthday to me!

The next day is sailing through the Franz Josef Land archipelago. We get off at an Island by paddleboat, the island shore crowded with giant walruses with their Sabre teeth and above them on the glacier cliff, walked an arctic fox. On another island, thousands of Fulmars, Kittiwake, Guillemots and Little Auks nest on exposed rocks. On the massive cliffs of another island, seabirds in their nests cover every inch of the elevation. They include Common Eider, Purple Sandpiper, Arctic Skua, Gulls and the famous Arctic Terns. I learn that these 30cm Arctic terns spend their spring and summer in the Arctic. It then flies 30,000km south to the Antarctic Circle, doing an Arctic-Antarctic round-trip migration yearly. Moving continually between Arctic and Antarctic summers, Arctic terns see more daylight than any other animal on Earth. Their love for travelling is way more than mine!

Then, as we sail through the wonderful vista of thick ice, with pools of clear blue water between the icepacks, an announcement comes on the tannoy - polar bear on the port side. We all rush to the deck, and only at a 40m distance, a majestic giant male bear hops from one ice pack to the other. Soon he leaves the area and is out of our sight.

The young Thai couple I had met the evening before joins me at dinner. As I return, filling my plate with fruits instead of desserts after the main course, the girl called Nan(cy) timidly asks if they could ask me for a favour. They said they were getting married on the North Pole. Then she surprises me by saying none of their families was with them and that would I mind giving her away at the ceremony. I reply at once it would be an honour.

Back at the badminton court, I learn my doubles partner for the last few days is the chief engineer of this nuclear-powered ship. On our return journey, he will show us around the ship's engine room. Life is full of surprises!

I retire to bed, the sun still up. But only after two hours announcement comes of more polar bear sightings. I rush out. Our ship had slowed down, and on the starboard side is a Polar bear mother with her cub, only 20m from the boat. The cute cub tries to jump between the ice packs, following its mother. Once, it almost falls into an ice pool. Mother looks back as the cub balances itself clumsily and follows - sumptuous. They hang around for some time as if giving everybody a chance to take photos.

Unfortunately, there is no satellite connection now, and no chance of watching the semi-final between England and Croatia, and not the final in a few days either! I return to my bed but cannot sleep.

The next afternoon, I wait for my turn, six at a time, for a helicopter ride. From above, an unbelievable scenery of pack ice as far as I can see to the horizon. And alone within the panorama of the white ice field is our red ship. A red speck, looking like a toy, deserted in an otherwise white wilderness of nothing else for hundreds of kilometres in all directions. We fly around for twenty minutes enjoying the incredible vista.

Onboard, we have an interesting lecture on sea ice and land ice. They ask for volunteers to join a group for ground research of the sea ice conditions around us on the way and at the North Pole. Satellites regularly collect data to monitor the polar condition, but only during these few voyages in the summer months could they corroborate their data with the findings on the ground. Twelve of us join.

Then a lovely barbecue on the rooftop. The outside temperature is -3°C, with wind chill probably a few degrees further down. But it is terrific; we all laugh and shiver at the same time.

The officers say we would reach the North Pole in the late evening today, in about 11-12 hours.

There is no time at the Poles, as time is calculated using longitude and all lines of longitude meeting at the poles. Scientists and explorers at the Poles record time-related data of their countries. As I talk to an Iranian family over a cup of coffee, an announcement comes of more bear sightings. We rush outside. There is a grand male Polar bear right next to our vessel. He is looking up and growling at the ship. As if to challenge – this is my territory, what do you think you are doing here? Awesome! We move on, leaving his kingdom.

North Pole: The entire ship is now buzzing with excitement. We would reach the North Pole in less than two hours. The pack-ice around us is not much different. Excitement is reaching its peak. There is no site marking or anything to point to the location of the North Pole. By calculating with onboard navigation equipment and computer with help from the satellite, they announce another ten minutes to go. We all rush out to the open deck.

The temperature outside is below -2°C, but no one cares. Anticipation reaches a climax as the counting starts - ten, nine, down to three, two - one. At 9-55pm Russian time, we are at the North Pole. Under a clear blue sky, the sun high up, we all shout, hug and kiss. Some wave flags. Champagne is served, and music is played. We dance and celebrate on top of the world! After countless photos, they announce it would be advisable to get some sleep for a few hours now. Tomorrow will be a big day on the grounds of the North Pole.

The following day, 14th July, Saturday, is cloudy outside. The expedition team had put a large flag to mark the site of the North Pole. We stand on 2-3m thick ice above a 4000m deep ocean. Any direction I look from here is south! We take pictures and then stand in a circle around the North Pole flag for one minute of silence in memory of anybody or anything we wanted. I think about my first daughter, who sadly departed us at thirty-one years of age, and how she would have reacted to this geographical and ecological marvel site. Then, still holding hands, we dance around the top of the globe celebrating anything we want! I remember all the amazing memory she had left for me in her brief life.

There is a choice of going for a plunge in a pool or a hike. I choose the latter. Fifteen of us slosh through the sea ice about 2km from the Pole. Two rangers join us with guns, one at the front and the other at the back. Although uncommon, stray Polar bears come around here searching for seals. As usual, I walk at the back of the line. After a while, the ranger in front asks everyone to stop and be quiet. With her binoculars, she has spotted a Polar bear at about 1km distance. Polar bears could run at a top speed of almost 40km per hour, slightly slower than Usain Bolt. We cut short our hike and return to the safety of our vessel.

Next is the time for the wedding. I, the proxy father, escort my 'daughter' Nan(cy) from the ship in her wedding dress, covered with a red Polar jacket at -1°C temperature. Groom with a few more passengers and the expedition leader was now waiting at the flag-marked site of the North Pole. Then, nearer the place, Nan throws off her jacket. My proxy daughter gives me a light hug, and I hand her over to her future husband for a brief ceremony presided by the expedition leader.

I miss my late daughter so much.

2018 Summer

I have finished writing the book the best I could. I have called it 'Indian immigrant' and sent it to Amazon for publishing from my laptop – a lot easier than going through other publishing routes. Now the time passes even more slowly. I look at the collection of old photographs on my laptop between checking the world cup football results. Looking at my first daughter's pictures makes me happy and sad at the same time. I know I will never see her again. She was not even thirty-two – too early to leave us forever.

My daughter and son-in-law come with some birthday cards made by my granddaughters. I ask to see their pictures and videos on their iPad. They look so grown up. My daughter tells me that they will be starting nursery school next month. So much I wish I could see them, but I understand that it may be too traumatic for them to see someone like me completely paralysed. Soon the nurses and others in the ward come with the birthday cake my daughter has made. They all sing me happy birthday and ask me to blow out the candle. I manage to blow out the single candle and secretly wish not to live another birthday.

A week later, my daughter comes with a parcel from Amazon for me. I ask her to open it and enjoy the surprise on her face when she finds the print copy of the book I have been writing without her knowledge. Then she is even more surprised when she opens the book and finds the dedication of my book to her and her departed sister. Tears flow from our eyes.

Then she tells me about her final exam coming up in a few months. Once she passes this exam and completes her training, she can become a consultant surgeon. I tell her I have no doubt that she would do well in her exam. I remind her that she had always excelled in any challenges. Then she tells me, timidly, that she was thinking of going abroad for a fellowship next year when she finishes her training here. Without that, a chance of getting a decent job in her speciality was not very likely. I tell her that she must do it. It will be not only her dream but mine too, to see her successful in her life.

The next time she comes, we talk about my granddaughter doing naughty things these days, and I remind my daughter of all the naughty things she and her sister did when they were growing up. Then I show her some of their old photos on my laptop. Before she leaves, I ask her to arrange for a solicitor to come to me. She looks surprised but, as always, does not ask why.

The solicitor comes with my daughter almost three weeks later. It has taken a while to find a suitable date for the solicitor and my daughter from her hospital work to come together during the daytime. After greeting the solicitor, I tell him I want to make a will. I explain to him that when I die, I would like any money left in my accounts and savings to be divided into three parts. It must be divided equally between two international charities, one for children, the other for maternal care, and a UK charity for the homeless. My daughter listens silently. The solicitor asks for more details before leaving and promises to return the following week.

The following week the solicitor returns with one of his colleagues and my daughter. He reads the will while I read it on my laptop from the email file he had sent me earlier. I confirm to him that this is what I want. Then he signs the will with his colleague with the ward sister as a witness. He leaves after a while, promising to send my daughter the documents by post with his bill. My daughter and I talk about my grandchildren starting nursery school in a couple of weeks, and I remember when we took her to nursery school many years back.

The consultant comes in the middle of the following week for his grand round with several doctors and nurses. When he asks me how I was doing, I request to talk to him with the ward sister alone for a few minutes. He looks at his watch and says it would be best if he could come back about an hour later when he has finished his rounds. Later, he returns with the ward sister. I explain to him clearly that I want to stop receiving any form of treatment with effect immediately.

They are stunned at first. But after a while, the consultant asks why and if I have discussed this with my daughter. I explain that I do not want to carry on any longer and this is my personal decision, although I will tell my daughter when she comes next time. After a few minutes of discussion, they record it on my notes and leave me alone.

When the nurses bring my lunch, I refuse it and say I don't want any food or drink from now on. They try to persuade me, but I ask them gently to please leave me alone. Then I go back to check the old photos on my laptop. Memories flood back. And pictures are, fortunately, of all good memories – who photographs bad experiences anyway?

My daughter arrives late in the evening. The hospital team must have informed her. She looks shattered – probably a mixture of her long workday and the news of my decision. Her eyes flood into tears as she holds my hand. After a while, she asks me why. I explain that I want to leave with good memories and don't want to linger to gradually waste away.

The next evening my daughter arrives again looking devastated. She knows I have been without food or drink for over twenty-four hours. She holds my hand and says she only heard earlier in the day that a place in one of the care homes outside the city may be available in a few weeks. I tell her it will not make any difference to me, and my decision remains unchanged.

My daughter, sometimes with my son-in-law, has been coming every evening after work for the last couple of days. At my request, they show me pictures and videos of my granddaughters. I share pictures with them of my two beloved daughters growing up on my laptop and try to bring some smiles to my only daughter's face but without luck.

I can feel my voice going down; the laptop sometimes does not understand my command, and I need to repeat it.

I don't believe in the afterlife neither did my first daughter. But now, at times, I wish there was an afterlife, even for a brief period, so I could see her lovely smile at least once more and get the tightest hug she always gave.

She -- was --- the best ---- hugger -- in --- the -- world.

------- ------ ---- -- -

Author bio

'I am a part of all that I have met' –
Ulysses (Tennyson)

Born in Joteram village, West Bengal, India, Biku Ghosh worked in the UK as a specialist surgeon for over forty years. Apart from travelling to over seventy-five countries on all seven continents, he has worked as a volunteer in twelve countries on five continents. While continuing with his international volunteering, currently, he also regularly works as a community volunteer.

Biku was earlier awarded OBE in recognition of his Wales-based teams' efforts in building and developing health links with Africa, with Ethiopia in particular. But as a strong critic of imperialism's historical, cultural, and political contexts and its international legacy, he later decided to return the honour given out in the name of a non-existent empire.

His first book, 'Indian Immigrant', historical fiction about how colonialism powerfully altered what being 'Indian' meant culturally and legally in Britain for the immigrants, was published in 2018. His travel memoir 'Around the world in 65 years' was published in 2020. His last book for young adults, 'How did it all start? Where did we come from?' includes the origin of our universe, the evolution of life and the human journey on earth, plus 48 creation stories from our ancestors from every continent.

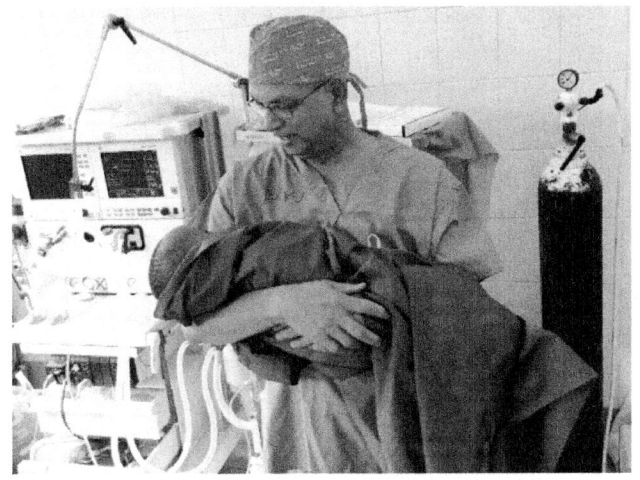

Email- Bikughosh@gmail.com

Facebook – biku.ghosh.75   Twitter - @GhoshBiku

Instagram – bikughosh7 and bookbiku

Acknowledgements

I am indebted to hundreds of people and their families across five continents who have kindly shared their life stories with me over the years.

I am also grateful to the Ivybridge Community Volunteers group for allowing me to work with them over the years and for giving me the opportunity to know the local families with people suffering from dementia and other disabilities. Similarly, I am grateful to the Leonard Cheshire Disability support group for allowing me to work with people with severe disabilities in one of their care homes in Llanhennock, Wales, in the past.

I am delighted that Alzheimer's Society (UK Registered Charity No 296645) has agreed for me to support their valuable work in raising awareness and supporting families with dementia sufferers through the sale of this book.

I really appreciate the opportunity free website Canva.com offered for me, a non-professional, to create my book cover with my own photos.

Finally, I thank Amazon KDP for publishing this book on their platform.

'We looked for workers. We got people instead.' - Max Frisch

This historical fiction tells stories of Indian immigrants to Britain over the last four centuries, not as an offshoot of race relations but from their lived perspectives.

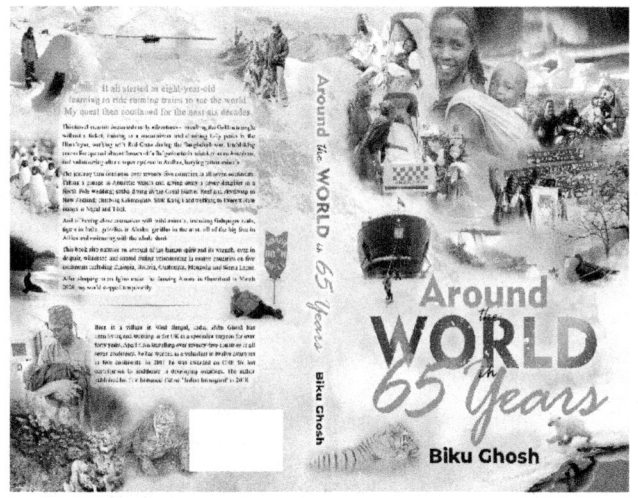

A memoir of travel on seven continents: climbing mountains, visiting Antarctica, the North Pole, & Galapagos. Also, about sharing the human spirit during volunteering in twelve countries on five continents.

The title says it all, plus 48 creation stories from our ancestors from six continents. Also, some interesting facts about Antarctica.

Printed in Great Britain
by Amazon